# Frozen!
## *A WWII Tail of Mind Over Matter*

By
Tom Patrick McAuliffe

NEXT STOP PARADISE
PUBLISHING
Ft. Walton Beach, Florida USA

# Frozen!
## *A WWII Tail of Mind Over Matter*

# <u>Dedication</u>

To my wife Sharon
and to my Grandpa

For the Greatest Generation
and anyone who served our nation

**<u>Profits from this book will be donated to
the WWII Museum, New Orleans, LA</u>**

# TABLE OF CONTENTS

# PREFACE

Few topics have inspired more books than World War II. Being Irish, story telling was central to my growing up and I remember sitting on my Grandpa's lap and listening. (By-the-way discover the inspiring story of my Grandpa, in the award winning book 'Mr. Mulligan: Champion Armless Golfer Tommy McAuliffe'.) Sitting in his old, creaky chair, Grandpa would regale me, his wide-eyed grandson, with tales of bravery in WWII.

As the flickering fire cast shadows on his weathered face, he spoke of heroic men enduring cold, sleepless nights in foxholes, and the camaraderie of soldiers who became brothers. The relentless hope that carried them through the darkest days seemed to be his focus. Grandpa's voice grew quieter as he recounted the moments of unexpected human kindness amidst the chaos, like sharing a meal with a local family or the sheer happiness of a solider receiving a letter from home. Despite the clouded eyes of age, his grandfather's mixture of pride and sorrow still shone through, leaving his grandson with a deep admiration for their sacrifices and determination.

Grandpa believed that the mind's power directly influenced happiness, success, and personal destinies. Among his favorite stories, was the one about Sgt. James Donovan of the 101st Airborne. He hailed from Ohio, and as you'll soon discover, it's an exceptionally captivating story. This story, whether true or an urban legend, highlights the astounding potential of the human mind. "Others are gonna believe about you what <u>you</u> believe about you!" Grandpa would often say. "The only handicap is the one within your own mind."

The preservation of the World War II soldiers' legacy is imperative for honoring their fight against unprecedented global tyranny. The sacrifices, bravery, and persistence they showed in the face of unimaginable hardship remind us of the price of freedom and the risks of aggression.

By preserving their stories, we pay tribute to their contributions, educate future generations about the atrocities of war, and emphasize the importance of peace and justice. By remembering, we cultivate gratitude and respect, allowing us to carry forward the lessons from their experiences in our present and for the future.

They are truly…

'The Greatest Generation!'

*Tom*

Fall 2024

# FOREWORD

To help illustrate his point about mind over matter, my Grandpa would always share and tell the story about a visit he made to talk with returning war troops at a large Army VA hospital after the war.

During the visit, he met a young Staff Sergeant of the United States Army who called him aside and told him the following story... A member of his outfit, Sgt. James Donovan of the Airborne, Rangers had gotten stranded behind enemy lines in Italy and, in trying to make his way back to his unit, he jumped onboard a Nazi freight train, hopefully headed in the right direction. The boxcar seemed completely new and was adorned with swastikas, giving him confidence that he would be overlooked if he hid inside.

While the train cars bumped along the tracks, his boxcar's sliding door abruptly slammed shut and locked. The boxcar was one of the new refrigerated 'icebox on wheels' that the innovative Nazi Army was using to move meats, poultry and produce to the troops in the southern regions of the Reich.

War is a relentless and unforgiving force that engulfs everything in its path. The landscape becomes a wasteland, marked by craters and debris, where the very air feels charged with tension and fear. In the thick of it, the line between humanity and chaos blurs with the noise of gunfire and explosions, creating a deafening symphony of destruction. It's also hard to get a hot meal!

Soldiers move through this hellish terrain with a mix of determination and dread, their minds steeled against the horrors they witness and partake in. Each day is a test of endurance, where the goal is not just to defeat the enemy but to survive and protect the comrades who have become like family. Yet, even in the darkest moments, flickers of humanity persist—a shared laugh, a gesture of kindness, a memory of home. These small acts of defiance against the overwhelming violence offer glimpses of hope and remind those caught in the conflict of what they fight for. It's a paradox of destruction and survival, loss and hope. And food helps keep moral high.

Whether true or simply war time urban legend, this story's point about the power of the human mind still rings true. Can a young soldier's mind kill him? The story of Sgt. James Donovan exemplifies two important things; one is that the human mind exerts tremendous control over our bodies and the other is the courage and determination of World War II's US Airborne soldiers. The Allied victory owes much to their contributions… their bravery and ferociousness continue to be remembered.

# CHAPTER 1

## Uncle Sammy
### *"Stand At Attention!"*

*"We shall fight on the beaches, we shall fight on the landing grounds, we shall fight in the fields and in the streets, we shall fight in the hills; we shall never surrender!"*
Sir Winston Churchill

James 'Jimmy' Donovan was born in the small town of Albian, in the middle of Ohio farm country. His upbringing during the Great Depression shaped him, fostering a strong sense of duty and a solid character. Because his father had served in the military during World War I, he instilled in his son a profound respect for the armed forces and a deep love for his country. When the United States entered World War II because of the attack on Pearl Harbor, Jimmy, along with many other young men of his generation, felt an overwhelming desire and need to serve our country. He joined the United States Army, without the consent of his parents, when he was just twenty years old. He's smart, good looking and he was sort of a smart aleck but with a great sense of humor. People always liked him.

While Jimmy Donovan was gazing at the rolling fields of Ohio corn that stretched out all the way to the horizon, he was standing on the porch. The farmhouse had belonged to his family since the early 1900's. By 1943, the entire world was engaged in war. Right from the beginning he understood it was time for him to join the struggle. He'd heard tales about the special Army Airborne units known as Paratroopers, who'd jump out of planes and land behind enemy lines gaining an advantage. He couldn't contain his excitement at the prospect of joining these elite armed forces. Shortly after he joined the Army he was ordered to Airborne school to try and earn his silver 'Ranger' wings. The routines, training regimens, and personal experiences of military service would shape Jimmy, and countless others like him, in preparation for one of the most important times in history. He was one of millions thru 'Boot Camp' and he was anxious for it all to get underway. He wanted the opportunity to do his small part.

Jimmy Donovan stepped onto the green bus and was greeted by a gentleman wearing a peculiar hat that looked like Smoky the Bear. The guy seemed upset and communicated with him exclusively via screaming. When he arrived at the induction center for the United States Army as part of the initial screening, they put recruits through a series of medical examinations to determine fitness for duty. After completing the basic medical examinations, the doctors tested James' vision and hearing, checked his blood pressure, and examined him for any physical problem that could disqualify him from service. The doctors then administered a series of immunizations to safeguard him against diseases common in the various theaters of conflict overseas. He felt like a pin cushion!

Recruits like Donovan were required to take part in Basic Training, which was sometimes referred to as 'Boot Camp' or 'Basic'. This rigorous curriculum prepares them for active duty service. The training may last anywhere from eight to twelve weeks, and its primary objective is to impart discipline, physical conditioning, and fundamental combat skills. The training routine breaks down into various phases, with each phase focusing on a particular component of military readiness.

During 'Basic', the daily program was a tough and organized routine. The wake-up call, known as reveille, sounded at five AM sharp, and the troops were expected to wake up, dress, and prepare for the day within five minutes.

Physical training (PT) was the first activity of the day, and it comprised a variety of strengthening and endurance-building exercises from running to calisthenics, and other similar activities. Following PT, the soldiers would eat breakfast, and then they would engage in a full day of training activities.

The foundation of the training was the development of physical fitness by running for extended distances and completing obstacle

*Items from Basic... Maps, Compass, whistle, etc.*

courses. The goal was to make certain that every soldier could endure the physical demands of combat, whether it was marching long miles while carrying heavy packs and weapons or fighting with hand-to-hand combat in the middle of the night.

"I found strength and muscles I didn't even know I had," Jimmy told his Mom afterward. "And I like the structure of boot camp but we want it to be over soon... we're itching to get over there and give the Krauts the business end of our M1s!" he said. 'And every time I would get mad at the Drill Instructors I would realize that they were just tryin to save my life by giving me the combat skills I'd need. Some of them are a real pain tho..." he explained. "If everything goes well over the next few weeks I'll be off to Jump School and the Airborne Rangers!" he said.

In the military, 'drill and ceremony' are a large part of maintaining discipline and learning to work together as a team. James and his fellow recruits, devoted a significant amount of time to mastering the skills of marching in formation, performing precise movements with his rifle, and following directions immediately and without question. Through participation in these exercises, recruits develop a sense of cohesiveness and discipline, learning how to move and behave as a single unit. The repetitious nature of drill and ceremony also imprints a sense of obedience and respect of authority. It works for 99.9% of soldiers.

During Boot Camp, instruction in weaponry is among the most vital training components. In short order Jimmy became proficient in the handling, maintenance, and firing of a wide variety of weapons, one of which being the M1 Garand rifle, the standard weapon issued to Army infantrymen. On the rifle range, Donovan spent a significant amount of time honing his marksmanship skills and gaining an understanding of the principles of sighting, shooting, and reloading. He became a natural. Besides the M1, training in using various other weapons, like bayonets, grenades, bazookas and machine guns is done. Tools of the trade.

Field Training Exercises, known as FTXs, simulate combat conditions and test the recruits' ability to apply what they learn in the classroom. Recruits performed mock battles, patrols, and defensive operations during these drills, which frequently took place in difficult-to-navigate terrain. Using maps and compasses, Jimmy and his fellow soldiers rehearsed digging foxholes, setting up camps, and navigating through unknown countryside. During these drills, they became better prepared to deal with the unpredictability and terrible conditions faced on the battlefields of Europe or the Pacific.

Basic Army education also includes several essential components of tactical training. Jimmy gained knowledge of small unit tactics, which includes the ability to move as a squad, set up ambushes, and carry out reconnaissance missions along with other skills. Besides that, the instructors taught him how to conceal and camouflage himself, and the importance of maintaining stealth during military operations. Throughout tactical training, the instructors strongly emphasized rapid thinking, adaptability, and unit cooperation.

Besides the physical and field training they include classroom instruction on military conventions, history, and tactics. In the lectures that Jimmy attended, they covered several subjects, including military law, first aid, and the Geneva POW Convention. Besides this, he gained knowledge regarding the organizational structure of the Army and the many roles and responsibilities that are associated with the various grades and units. Understanding the larger context of his service and the significance of his function within the military was necessary for becoming a good solider.

The Army's basic training turned out to be anything but a game of fun. Being away from his family and friends for the first time in his young life caused Donovan to experience a variety of negative emotions, including depression, physical tiredness, mental stress, and emotional pressure. To prepare the recruits for the harsh reality of war, the drill instructors were extremely demanding and severe, pushing them to their absolute limits. As he was under continual pressure to perform at his best, Jimmy had to overcome his limits. The recruits developed a sense of hardness and determination because of these challenges, which also helped them form close bonds with each other.

One of the most important components of basic training was the development of a sense of brotherhood and camaraderie among the

*Basic Training with various weapons*

*General McAuliffe addresses the troops before a jump.*

individuals who were training to become soldiers. The shared experience of overcoming obstacles and working together towards a common goal built relationships between the individuals. The sense of brotherhood and mutual support that existed among the members of the unit made maintaining morale and cultivating a sense of unity inside the unit possible. A team mentality was the goal.

The graduation ceremony was the completion of basic training. During this ceremony, Jimmy and his fellow recruits were now officially acknowledged as real soldiers. His ceremony signified his transfer from recruit to active duty and it was a moment of pride and triumph for him. Also for his parents, who traveled for 18 hours all the way from Ohio on the Greyhound Bus to be there. The Army delivered his assignment instructions to Airborne Jump School just after he graduated from Basic. By making it through Boot Camp he gained the knowledge and experience needed for survival, at least he hoped so.

In the future when he thought back about his time in Basic, Donovan realized the significant influence that it had already exerted on his journey through life. The intense training, discipline, and feeling of purpose turned him from a civilian into a soldier. He was now prepared to confront the enemy and the reality of battle... at least that is what he believed. In the course of his military career, he would carry with him the lessons he'd learned and the relationships he had built there. Jimmy knew that the experiences he had were not just about getting ready for war, but also about developing his overall character. His ability to bounce back from adversity was also enhanced.

And Donovan was part of the best equipped Army in history! He glanced around at the other men in his unit, each of them similarly laden with equipment, their faces set with the same determined grimace. Carrying a pack is a burden all soldiers share, a constant reminder of the task ahead and being well prepared.

His rifle, the M1 Garand, was his most trusted companion. Weighing just over nine pounds, it was an instrument of war that could fire eight rounds of .30-06 Springfield ammunition in rapid succession. Jimmy had spent countless hours training with it, learning to clean and maintain it as if it were a part of himself. Slung over his shoulder, it provides a reassuring presence as a tool of survival. The bayonet, a 10-inch blade that attached to the muzzle of his rifle, hung in its scabbard at his side. An implement of close combat, it's a relic of wars gone by, yet still necessary in the trenches and foxholes where enemies might suddenly appear.

In his haversack (the Army term for a small backpack), neatly organized despite the haphazard nature of its contents, were 'K-rations'. Packaged in small, waxed cardboard boxes, these food rations were meant to sustain him through the rigors of battle. Each box contained a canned meat product, biscuits, a fruit bar, a packet of powdered beverage, and a small piece of chewing gum. It wasn't much, and it certainly wasn't tasty, but it provided the nutrients needed to keep going.

Strapped to the side of the haversack was his US Army entrenching tool—a small, collapsible shovel. Jimmy had learned to dig quickly and efficiently, creating foxholes and trenches that would offer some measure of protection from the enemy's fire. The tool was also useful for other tasks like clearing debris.

The gas mask, carried in a separate canvas bag, was a grim reminder of the horrors of chemical warfare from WW1. It was bulky and uncomfortable, but its presence was necessary. The memory of mustard gas from the Great War loomed large in the minds of the military planners, determined that their soldiers would be well prepared for such an attack.

Attached to his belt were two canteens, each filled with precious water. In the heat of battle, hydration was essential, and every drop was a lifeline. Beside them, his first aid pouch contained bandages, sulfa powder to prevent infection, and morphine syringes for pain—a small but essential kit that could mean the difference between life and death on the battlefields of war.

Jimmy's Army uniform, made of heavy wool, was both a shield and a burden. It protected him from the elements but could become stifling in the heat of summer or soak through in the rain. His helmet, an M1 steel pot, sat snugly on his head, its weight a constant presence. Inside, a liner provided some comfort, nut it's the outer shell that might deflect shrapnel offering a fragile promise of safety.

Every item he carried had a purpose, every ounce was accounted for. The combined weight of his gear was a testament to the demands of modern warfare, a physical manifestation of the strategy and planning that went into each soldier's role. As Jimmy Donovan marched onward, he knew that the equipment on his back was as vital to his survival as his training and courage. The burden was heavy, but it was one he bore with a sense of duty and resolve, each step bringing him closer to the front lines, the challenges that awaited and ultimately back home to Ohio.

Because of their participation in World War II, soldiers such as Donovan underwent a profound transformation. It was a period of time dedicated to putting young men through rigorous mental and physical tests to better prepare them for the brutal and bloody realities of combat. Jimmy became a skillful soldier who was prepared to serve his country. Because of his hard training, his commitment to discipline, and the creation of close ties with his fellow soldiers, the lessons gained should keep him from being killed.

Military leaders selected Private 'Jimmy' Donovan for the newly formed Airborne units, which were part of a bold and innovative military strategy involving deploying soldiers behind enemy lines via parachutes. The new Airborne training grounds were at Camp Toccoa, in Georgia. The sight of the towering Currahee Mountain greeted Jimmy when

he arrived, and it left a lasting impression on him. He was one of the many young guys who was eager to show their worth at the base, which was a bustling hub of activity. It was a whirlwind of paperwork, medical examinations, and challenges. The following morning, training would start in earnest and he was more than ready.

Reveille went off at precisely five o'clock in the morning, jolting Jimmy out of his bunk. Camp Toccoa was a hard place to spend one's time. Calisthenics, obstacle courses, and long runs up Currahee Mountain were all part of the rigorous physical training that was required. Because they were driven by the desire to earn their wings, Jimmy and the other recruits pushed themselves to their absolute limits. The drill instructors were strict and unyielding consistently demanding obedience and perfection.

The "Three Miles Up, Three Miles Down" run was one of the most grueling aspects of the training. During this strenuous workout, participants were required to run up and down Currahee Mountain, which served as a test of endurance that differentiated the strong from the weak. Through sheer determination and the support of his fellow soldiers, Jimmy somehow persevered through the immense pain he was experiencing.

After several weeks of rigorous physical training the time had come for 'Jump School'. In the beginning, Jimmy and his fellow soldiers took part in ground training to learn the fundamentals of parachuting. Through repeated practice, they perfected the skills of jumping from towers, including the correct exit, body position, and landings. In order to complete a jump successfully, the instructors emphasized the significance of overcoming or managing your fear.

The very first jump was an experience that was fraught with anxiety. Jimmy's heart was pounding intensely in his chest as the plane continued to ascend. The others were waiting for the green light, and he joined them in forming a line. After it arrived at the right spot in the air, he jumped into the void, and the strong wind blew past him. Instantaneously, the chute opened, and he floated in the air, with the ground rapidly approaching. He executed a perfect landing, exhilarated and relieved. Over the next few weeks, he completed five successful jumps and eventually earning the coveted silver wings of a paratrooper.

With basic airborne training completed, Jimmy and his unit moved on to advanced training. They learned about glider operations, demolitions, and hand-to-hand combat. Tactical exercises became more complex, simulating real combat scenarios. Jimmy's unit practiced night jumps, pathfinding, and establishing drop zones under fire. The emphasis was on teamwork, stealth, and adaptability. Difficult but worthy lessons.

One of the most intense training exercises involved a full-scale mock battle. Jimmy's unit, dropped miles behind 'enemy' lines, was tasked with capturing and holding a strategic position in one of the most intense exercises involving a full-scale mock battle. They moved through dense forests, setting up ambushes and avoiding detection. Jimmy's leadership and quick thinking earned him the respect of his comrades and the attention of his superiors. He was getting good at this.

From the moment Jimmy Donovan set foot in Airborne Ranger School, it was clear to him that the men around him were cut from two different cloths. Some had the raw confidence of those who seemed destined to come through the war unscathed, untouched by the violence and chaos that loomed on the horizon. These men moved with a certain ease, their smiles quick and carefree, as if they carried some secret assurance that luck would be on their side. They aced the grueling physical challenges with seeming effortlessness, their eyes bright with anticipation rather than dread. You just knew these guys were gonna make it thru without so much as a scratch!

In stark contrast were those men Jimmy instinctively knew were marked for a toe tag and body bag. Their fates were almost etched into their naïve expressions. They wore a sort of foreknowledge of their fates. These men approached every jump, every drill, with a dogged intensity, as if bracing themselves for the inevitable storm. Their camaraderie was quieter, more solemn. They shared knowing glances aware of the burdens they would soon carry and the new knowledge that death comes quick.

Jimmy found himself caught between these two worlds, observing with a mix of admiration and unease. He understood that war was an unpredictable beast, and there was no way to tell who would emerge unscathed and who would die. Yet, he couldn't help but feel that those who seemed resigned to their fate carried an attitude that might serve them well in the darkest of times. They were ready not just to fight but to endure. They were ready to face the horrors of war with a courage born not of confidence but of necessity. And in their quiet strength, Jimmy found a source of inspiration, a reminder that bravery lay in accepting the unknown and standing firm in faith both in God and in one's own abilities.

Jimmy Donovan and company stood at the edge of the tarmac, the distant hum of C-47 aircraft engines filling the air. The harsh reality of a world at war had drawn him here, to the center of the US Army Airborne School. Fort Benning was a far cry from his peaceful corn and dairy farm back in Ohio. The scorching humid heat of Georgia subjected Jimmy and his fellow recruits to its intensity as they waited in line for their first taste of airborne training. As they gathered together, the recruits could hear their instructor, a grizzled sergeant major with piercing blue eyes and a voice like gravel, as he talked.

"Greetings, Ladies, and welcome to Jump School!" he yelled. "In the coming weeks, you will gain the skills necessary to jump out of airplanes, land without incident, and fight like hell when you touch down on the ground. Some of you won't make it, those who do will be the world's finest combat soldiers. Anytime! Anywhere!"

It was hard but he pushed on, driven by the determination to earn those silver wings. Classes on parachute packing and airborne tactics followed, with Jimmy and his comrades painstakingly learning to fold and pack their chutes, each step critical to their survival.

As the days wore on, Jimmy faced his fears head-on. The 34-foot training towers loomed ominously, and the moment he first stepped off the platform felt like an eternity, his stomach lurching as he plummeted before the harness jerked him to a stop. Each jump from the tower built his confidence.

As the training at Camp Toccoa drew to a close, the reality of the upcoming deployment set in. The paratroopers were briefed on their mission in Europe, a critical part of the Allied invasion. Jimmy and his comrades spent hours studying and rehearsing their roles. They knew they would be among the first to land in occupied territory, paving the way for the main invasion force to arrive shortly thereafter. Letters from home became rarer and more precious, a connection to a world that seemed increasingly distant. Jimmy wrote to his family, assuring them he was ready and determined to do his duty. The bond with his fellow paratroopers grew stronger, a brotherhood forged in the fires of intense training and combat... something 'Rangers' carry for life. All the training and effort had led to this. And he felt ready.

The culmination of their training came with the first jump from a C-47. Jimmy stood in the cramped belly of the plane, the roar of the engines vibrating through his bones. His hands clenched the static line, knuckles white with tension. The jump-master's hand slapped his shoulder, and Jimmy stepped into the abyss. The rush of wind and the sudden, violent jerk of the parachute opening filled him with exhilaration and relief. Below him, the training field spread out like a patchwork quilt, and he steered his chute toward the drop zone, landing with a thud and triumph.

The last phase of their preparation took them into the woods for combat training. Here, they learned the brutal realities of war: how to move stealthily through enemy territory, set ambushes, and engage in hand-to-hand combat. And perhaps most importantly how to kill quickly and easily. The instructors, many of them veterans of battles in North Africa and Sicily, imparted their hard-earned wisdom, molding Donovan and his comrades into a cohesive and lethal unit. After Jump School he received advanced training at Fort Benning, Georgia. He successfully completed his training and Jimmy earned his silver wings joining the

506th Parachute Infantry Regiment of the 101st 'Screaming Eagles'.

As the day of deployment to Europe arrived, Jimmy felt a mixture of anticipation and anxiety. Letters from home warned of shortages and blackouts there and of neighbors and friends supporting the war effort by doing their part. He realized the importance of the task ahead and had come to grips with giving his life to rescue Europe from Nazi tyranny.

As the troop ship slowly made its way across the Atlantic watching for German U-Boats along the way, Jimmy and his platoon continued to train and plan. Once in England Jimmy and his unit met for a last briefing before D-Day. It was finally revealed that their exact destination would be Normandy on the coast of France. His mission: parachute behind the enemy line, secure key positions, and pave the way for the massive invasion force which followed. The night before the jump, they gathered around, sharing jokes, and stories. In the predawn darkness of June 6, 1944, Jimmy boarded a plane once more only this time, the stakes were real. Very real indeed.

# CHAPTER 2

## A Shooting War
### *Over there...*

*"I've been around, ya know? There was a time I could see. And I have seen. Boys like these, younger than these, their arms torn out, their legs ripped off. But there is nothing like the sight of an amputated spirit. There's no prosthetic for that."*
Lt. Col. Frank Spade, USA

Time had passed quickly and he found himself on the other side of the Atlantic pond. It was Monday, June 5, 1944, the night before historic D-Day. Jimmy stood on an airfield in England, geared up and ready for the most critical mission of his young life. Tensions were palpable as he and his fellow paratroopers loaded onto the Douglas C-47 'Skytrain' aircraft. The plane roared to life, and soon they were airborne, flying across the English Channel towards France, Europe and Nazis.

The jump into the landing zone was chaotic and harrowing. Anti-aircraft fire filled the night sky, and the planes swerved violently. When the green light finally came on, Jimmy and his comrades jumped into the dark, moonless night. The drop zone was a scene of total confusion, with paratroopers scattered far and wide. Jimmy landed in a field, quickly gathered his gear, and set off to

find his unit. After the jump, the soldiers experienced intense fighting and strategic maneuvering for hours. The aim was to secure key bridges and crossroads, disrupting the enemy and aiding the invasion forces to come. Jimmy's unit encountered heavy resistance, but their training and determination paid off. They held their positions, repelling counterattacks and capturing critical Nazi strong points. The sense of accomplishment was immense, but there was little time to rest. The war for Normandy had only just started, and Jimmy knew that the coming days would bring much greater hardships.

The success of airborne operations on D-Day was a first turning point in the war, but it was only the beginning. Jimmy and his battalion continued to fight through the hedgerows of Normandy, facing severe resistance from the 'Wehrmacht' (the German Army). Daily tests of guts and skill challenged the paratroopers. He knew the road ahead was uncertain, but he was ready to face whatever came, alongside his brothers in arms.

Jimmy Donovan rubbed his almost bald head and adjusted the weight on his shoulders, the canvas straps of his 'Solider's Burden' were digging into his flesh. The Haversack, was packed tightly with everything he might need—or at least, everything the Army believed he might need. He glanced around at the other men in his unit, each of them similarly laden, their faces set in stone. They loss 3 during the jump; Jones, Haggerty and Hunter.

His rifle, an M1 named 'Peggy', was now his most trusted companion. Weighing just over nine pounds, it was an instrument of death that could fire eight rounds of .30-06 Springfield ammunition in rapid succession. Donovan had spent countless hours training with it, learning to clean and maintain it as if it were a part of himself. Slung over his shoulder, it provided a reassuring presence, a tool of survival and a means of defense. His bayonet, a 10-inch blade that attached to the muzzle of his rifle, hung in its scabbard at his side. It was an implement of close combat, a relic of wars gone by, yet still necessary in the trenches and foxholes where enemies might suddenly appear and it was a good all purpose tool.

In his haversack, neatly organized despite the variety of its contents, was some 'K-rations'. Packaged in small, waxed cardboard boxes, these food rations were meant to sustain him through the rigors of battle. Each box contained a canned meat product, biscuits, a fruit bar, a packet of powdered beverage, and a small piece of chewing gum. It wasn't much, and it certainly wasn't tasty, but it provides the calories and nutrients needed for troops to keep going.

Strapped to the side of the haversack was his entrenching tool—a small, collapsible shovel.

Jimmy had learned to dig quickly and efficiently, creating foxholes and trenches that would offer some measure of protection from the enemy's fire. The tool was also useful for many other tasks.

The gas mask, carried in a separate canvas bag, was a grim reminder of the horrors of chemical warfare. It was bulky and uncomfortable, but its presence was necessary. The memory of mustard gas from WW1 loomed large in the minds of the military planners, and they were determined that their soldiers would be prepared for such an attack.

Attached also to his belt were two canteens, each filled with precious water. In the heat of battle, hydration was crucial, and every drop was a lifeline. Beside them, his first aid pouch contained bandages, sulfur powder to prevent infection, and morphine for pain—a small but essential kit could mean the difference between life and death.

Jimmy's uniform, made of heavy wool, was both a shield and a burden. It protected him from the elements but could become stifling in the heat of summer or soak through in the rain. His helmet, an M1 steel pot, sat snugly on his head, its weight a constant presence. Inside, a liner provided some comfort, but it was the outer shell offering a fragile promise of comfort and safety.

As the French coast came into view, he steadied his breath and focused on the mission ahead. The red light turned green at the door of the aircraft, and he leapt into history. The moonless sky over Normandy was filled with thousands of paratroopers, their chutes blossoming in the night sky. Jimmy landed hard and with his training kicking in he assembled with his platoon. The fight for Europe had begun in earnest, and Donovan, now a semi-seasoned Airborne Paratrooper, was more than ready to fight.

The first significant encounter that he had in combat was during the Allied invasion on D-Day. The mission was a component of 'Operation Overlord', the most extensive amphibious attack in US Army history. In the early hours of the morning, Donovan and his fellow paratroopers were dropped behind enemy lines and were given the mission of seizing critical bridges and highways in order to prevent German reinforcements from reaching the beaches where Allied troops were about to land. The largest armada of war ships was just off shore and ready.

*A lone Paratrooper marches back to the LZ.*

Tracers and anti-aircraft fire lighted the night as Jimmy fell through the dark sky. He soon rejoined other paratroopers after landing in a field close to the French town of Caen, his ultimate destination. Although the drop had dispersed the units in a broad area, Jimmy's training kicked in and amid the mayhem, he help secure the town and disrupt Nazi operations. They were very successful.

In the aftermath of the successful completion of D-Day, the commanders assigned the mission of seizing the town of Carentan to the 101st Airborne Division. This objective was vital as it would connect the American troops located at Utah and Omaha Beaches. The paratroopers were up against experienced German soldiers that were well-entrenched, and the battle was harder than anticipated. Despite being under heavy fire, Donovan showed an extraordinary amount of bravery as he moved across the hedgerows and fields of Normandy. Despite suffering the death of a significant number of soldiers, the 101st successfully seized the town of Carentan after many days of intense fighting, strengthening the Allied footing in France and Europe and leading to its ultimate victory.

During the fall of 1944, Donovan, who'd now been promoted to the rank of Sergeant, played an active role in 'Operation Market Garden,' an ambitious plan to seize several bridges in the Netherlands and establish a passageway into German territory. Bridges and rail heads were to be taken by the 101st as part of their mission. Because of the fierce resistance from the Germans and the difficulties in logistics, their missions eventually failed and the Nazis had some initial successes.

The conditions that Jimmy's regiment was subjected to were extremely harsh, involving intense artillery and machine-gun fire. He was a first-hand witness to the atrocities that were committed throughout the war. One day he watched as the Nazi SS interrogated and then, for no apparent reason, shot one of his buddies in the head and then the Nazis stood around laughing. He'd make them pay for that! Over the next few months the Airborne forces had became recognized for their tenacity and perseverance. They simply refused to give up, maintaining their position in the face of numerous counterattacks by the enemy.

During the Allied invasion, Donovan had his first significant experience in killing. The mission was a component of 'Operation Overlord', which was the most extensive amphibious attack in the nation's history. In the early hours of the morning, they dropped him and his fellow paratroopers behind enemy lines with the mission of securing key bridges and roads in order to prevent German reinforcements from reaching the beaches where Allied forces were going to land later that day. The young Nazi solider poked his head up from behind a bush and Donovan promptly shot him dead.

It was his first night in France and the sky was a deep, inky black, the stars obscured by thick clouds promising rain. Sgt. Jimmy Donovan and his buddy Private Tom Harris from Michigan sat in their foxhole in the shadows of their makeshift camp. The distant rumble and flashes of artillery are a constant reminder of the war that surrounds

A German Solider

them. The night was eerily quiet, the usual banter among the men muted by the weight of what had occurred earlier as well as their upcoming mission.

Harris broke the silence first, his voice barely more than a whisper. "You ever get used to it, Jimmy? The fear, the killin and the waitin?"

Jimmy shook his head, his eyes scanning the horizon for the enemy as if searching for answers in the darkness. "No, ya don't. Waiting's the hardest part for me... too much time to think!"

Harris nodded, fiddling with the strap of his helmet. "I keep thinking about what's next!"

42

Jimmy turned to look at him directly, his expression serious. "Yeah, it's gonna be tough. But we've got a job to do. We've got to take out that machine gun nest, tank, whatever. If we don't do our job, lotta good men are gonna die trying to push through those enemy lines," he said.

Harris swallowed hard, his adam's apple bobbing in the dim light. "I know. It's just... I can't stop thinking about what might happen. What if I freeze up? What if I just can't do it?" he asked.

Jimmy placed a reassuring hand on Harris's shoulder. "You won't freeze up, Harris. I've seen you in action. You're one of the best shots in the unit. Just remember your training and stay focused. We all got each other's backs out there. Right?"

Harris nodded, taking a deep breath. "Thanks, Jimmy. It helps knowing you're here. You always seem so cool and calm. You're the bees knees!"

Jimmy chuckled softly, a sound actually devoid of humor. "Calm? I'm scared as shit too, Harris. Anyone who says they're not is either lying or a fool. But fear keeps us sharp. Makes us careful. We just can't let it control us," he said.

Harris looked down, his fingers tracing patterns in the dirt. "I keep thinking about home. My mom, my little sister. I promised them I'd come back."

Jimmy's eyes softened. "We all have someone waiting for us, that's why we fight. To get back home and to make sure people like your mom and sister don't ever have to see this hell. Ever."

The sound of footsteps approached, and both men turned to see Lt. Anderson standing there in the dark, his face etched with determination. "Briefing is five, gentlemen. Get your gear ready!"
Jimmy nodded, rising to his feet. "Yes, sir." He turned back to Harris, helping him up. "Let's do this, Harris. For them."

Harris took a deep breath, "For them!"

They gathered their gear, the weight of their next mission settling over them like a shroud. As they moved toward the briefing area, Jimmy glanced at Harris and offered a small, encouraging smile.

"Remember, one step at a time. We'll get through this together," he said.

Harris returned the smile, a spark of determination in his eyes. "Together!"

The men joined the others, the camaraderie and shared purpose unspoken but deeply felt. They listened intently as Lt. Anderson outlined the mission, each detail committing to memory, each step an important part of their success. And as they prepared to face the enemy, the bond between them strengthened, forged in the fires of war and the promise of survival.

In the aftermath of a successful D-Day, the 101st Airborne was given the mission of seizing and securing the town of Carentan, which was a large objective that would connect the American forces at Utah and Omaha Beaches. The paratroopers were up against experienced German combat soldiers that were well-entrenched. Despite suffering the death of dozens of soldiers, the 101st successfully seized Carentan after days of intense fighting strengthening the Allied footing in France.

In September 1944, Donovan took part in 'Operation Market Garden', an ambitious plan to secure a series of bridges in the Netherlands and create a pathway into Germany. Because of the fierce resistance from the Germans and the difficulties in logistics, the mission eventually failed. His unit faced brutal conditions, including heavy artillery and machine-gun fire. He was a first-hand witness to the atrocities that were committed throughout the war, but he also observed the heroics and friendship of his fellow troops. The airborne had gained a reputation for unwavering determination and undeniable guts.

Donovan's participation in the Battle of the Bulge, during the winter of 1944-1945, was one of the most rigorous experiences he'd ever had. The German army conducted an unexpected attack in the Ardennes Forest in Belgium, which resulted in a bulge in the front lines of the Allied forces. Under the direction of General Tony McAuliffe, who famously said, 'Nuts!' to the Germans, the 101st Airborne quickly transported itself to the town of Bastogne, an important crossroads in Belgium. Cold weather, no supplies, and unrelenting assaults were all things that Donovan and his fellow soldiers had to suffer while being surrounded and outnumbered.

The situation appeared to be extremely precarious, but the paratroopers failed to give in. A symbol of resistance, Jimmy's foxhole became a rallying point, and his rifle became a symbol of survival. The tenacity of the whole division, combined with the eventual arrival of General Patton's Third Army, turned the tide of the battle. Following the lifting of the siege, the defense of Bastogne, Belgium became a defining moment in the unit's illustrious history. Its tactics are taught even today. Following the lifting of the siege, the history of the defense of Bastogne became a defining moment in the long illustrious history of the 101st 'Screaming Eagles'. Jimmy was so proud.

Donovan's experience is typical of the daring and tenacity of the US Airborne troopers in World War

II. They were regular guys who confronted enormous trials and emerged as heroes. It's a monument to their bravery that their memory will live on as a testament to the fact that their sacrifices were vital in the triumph of the Allies.

# CHAPTER 3

## Bongiorno...Pasta or Bullets?
### *Italy Withdraws from Losing*

*A German messenger runs to Hitler and says
"Mein Fuhrer, Italy has joined the war!"
Hitler replies "Not to worry, send
one SS division to defeat them."
"No Mein Fuhrer they have joined our side."
"Damn, now we'll have to send 10 divisions
just to help them!"*

Many people consider the Battle of Monte Cassino, which took place in Italy from January to May of 1944, to be one of the most important conflicts in Italian history if not the entire war. In this series of four attacks on the German 'Winter Line,' the Allies' goal was to break through to Rome and take control of the situation and area. The conflict is significant for the violent combat that occurred, its strategic significance and the destruction of the historic medieval monastery that was at Monte Cassino.

"If it weren't for the war I'd be having a great time!" said Jimmy. "Italy is really beautiful and the local people have been really warm and welcoming. They're glad we're here. I had my first hot meal in a month from a local woman who

stopped me on the side of the road, dragged me to her partially bombed out house, fed me and then refused any sort of trade or payment. These folks are just super nice!" he said.

When the Allies arrived in Italy in early September 1943, their initial objective was to take Naples, and then they planned to move northward toward Rome. Despite their plans, German soldiers erected strong defensive positions along their Winter Line, notably in the valley near Monte Cassino. The area controlled the major approach to Rome via the Liri Valley. These positions were strategically important. One of the most important defensive positions was the monastery itself, established by Saint Benedict in the year 529 AD, it was on a hill overlooking the town and the valley that surrounds it. It was a perfect place to set up a defensive location as you had a 360 degree view.

However the Battle of Monte Cassino was not just one but actually comprised four distinct phases:

•The First Battle: January 17-22, 1944
The British X Corps was the one that started the initial attack. The goal was to break through the German lines that were along the Garigliano River. An additional Allied invasion, known as Operation

Shingle, was to take place at Anzio, and the goal there was to direct German forces away from that location. Although there was some initial success, the onslaught ultimately failed because of the fierce opposition from the Germans and the challenging terrain. Neither side was yielding.

•The Second Battle: February 15-18, 1944
During the second assault, the Allies concentrated their efforts on seizing control of the town of Cassino and the hills that around it. The disputed bombing of the Monte Cassino monastery on February 15 is the event that brought the most attention to this armed conflict. Because the Allies thought the Germans were to use the monastery as

a place of observation, they decided to demolish it by a huge aerial bombardment. They later discovered that the Germans had not occupied the monastery, even though they had demolished it. Instead, they had moved in after the bombing and used the remains as a defended position. The ground attack that followed was unsuccessful in capturing the prime locations.

•The Third Battle: March 15-23, 1944
It became an international affair! During the third attack, troops from New Zealand and India attempted to capture the town and the hills that around it. An intense air bombardment was the first step, which was then followed by infantry assaults. The Allies were once again unsuccessful in their attempt to penetrate the German lines, despite the fierce combat and terrible fatalities occurring on both sides. The Nazis were dug in and had no plans to vacate.

•The Fourth Battle: May 11-18, 1944
'Operation Diadem' was the name given to the last and conclusive attack. It was a concerted operation that involved numerous Allied forces; Polish II Corps, British XIII Corps, and the French Expeditionary Corps all launched simultaneous attacks on various areas of the German lines. After a difficult and brutal battle, the Poles, in particular, were instrumental in the successful capture of Monte Cassino itself. By the 18th of May, Polish soldiers had successfully hoisted their flag atop the

remains of the monastery, signaling the conclusion of the battle. The local population suddenly appeared and began to cheer the Allied troops.

When considered as a whole, the four fights had a considerable influence on the entire battle situation. The Nazis were on the run and now the Allies could make real progress towards Rome, which they freed on June 4, 1944. Their successful assault of Monte Cassino and their breach of the German defensive line made that possible but the fighting resulted in about 55,000 Allied casualties and 20,000 German casualties. It was one of the longest and bloodiest battles of the entire Italian Campaign if not the whole war.

Over the years many people have raised doubts regarding the need for the bombing of the Monte Cassino monastery and it was and is still a contentious and hotly disputed issue. The Battle of Monte Cassino's particular viciousness and overall difficulty due to the terrain characterized the whole Italian Campaign. It highlighted the intricacies and conflicts of decision-making during times of war, as well as the perseverance of the Allied troops in their efforts to overcome powerful German defenses. In addition, the fight highlighted the strategic significance of Italy within the larger framework of WWII Europe. The Allies were attempting to weaken the Axis forces and prepare the way for the ultimate liberation of Europe.

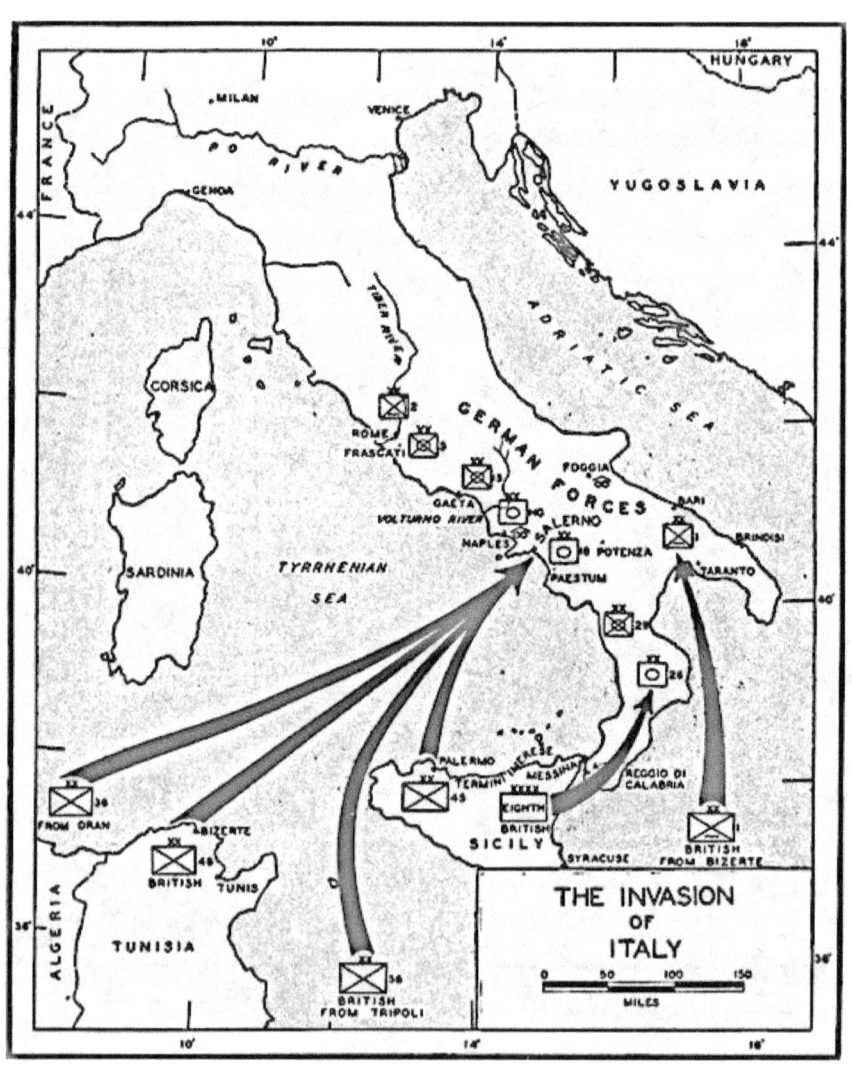

THE INVASION
OF
ITALY

0     50     100     150
MILES

# CHAPTER 4

## The Mission
### *Intel is Power*

*"Men, we're surrounded by the enemy. We have the greatest opportunity ever presented an Army. We can attack in any direction!"*
General Tony McAuliffe

Donovan woke up after grabbing 2 hours sleep following his 2-4am watch. It was daybreak and ten German armored divisions sporting the newly enhanced 'Tiger' Panzer tank (more armor and greater shot distance), as well as 25 elite Wehrmacht infantry divisions launched towards the Allied line. Sgt. Jimmy Donovan of Ohio and the US Army's elite 101st Airborne was right in the middle of all of it!

In the fall of 1944, Donovan, now with a field rank of Staff Sergeant, found himself in the heart of occupied Italy, a region of beautiful countryside, fields and farms now devastated by conflict. His battalion, the 5th Infantry Division, received a perilous mission: to disrupt German supply lines by targeting all key rail networks required to bring food and ammunition to the front. These rail lines were to either be liberated or destroyed and Jimmy was only to happy to oblige. He had always loved traveling by rail and had done so extensively. Jumping out of his plane the night air hit him hard.

Tracers and anti-aircraft fire illuminated the night sky as Donovan descended through the darkness. He soon rejoined with other paratroopers after landing in a field close to the town of Salerno, south of Naples, he'd reached his destination. The drop scattered the units widely, but his training kicked in and amid the mayhem, Donovan helped secure the town then totally disrupting military communications and ultimately preventing German reinforcements from joining the battle.

The chaos of the battlefield engulfed Jimmy, the world around him a maelstrom of noise, cries and smoke. He and one of his best friends, Charlie Shea, moved as one, a seamless partnership forged in countless skirmishes. Shea was always there, a steady presence under fire and like Harris was always by Jimmy's side. His grin could cut through even the darkest moments. As they pressed forward, there was a sudden, blinding flash of light, followed by an earth-shattering explosion that seemed to suck the air from Jimmy's lungs. The ground heaved beneath him, and he was thrown violently to the side, his ears ringing with a high-pitched whine.

For a moment, everything was surreal and suspended in slow motion, as if time itself had decided to take a break. The acrid smell of smoke and burnt flesh stung Jimmy's nose as he struggled to his knees, his head spinning. Panic clawed at him as he looked around, trying to make sense of the disarray. Then he saw the crater where Charlie had been standing just seconds before... the realization crashing over him with a force more powerful than any explosion. Shea had been vaporized! The spot was now just a hole, a smoking ruin with fragments of gear and debris scattered like ghosts of what had just been. The smoke of battle with the scent of death was all around and Donovan had a weird thought... how can you bury someone who was vaporized?

The air, thick with tension, saw Donovan and his fellow troops crouched behind the remnants of a crumbling stone wall. The early morning mist clinging to the ground like a shroud. The forest around them was eerily silent, the only sound the distant rustle of leaves whispering in the wind. Then, suddenly, the stillness shattered as the crack of gunfire erupted, a staccato burst that sent birds fleeing into the sky. Bullets whizzed past, snapping branches and kicking up dirt, and the American soldiers sprang into action, their training taking over in the chaos.

Jimmy pressed himself against the wall, his heart pounding in his chest, his senses acutely attuned to the pandemonium. He peered over the edge, squinting through the haze to locate the source of the attack. The Nazi forces were dug in across the clearing, their grey uniforms blending with the smoke and shadows. With a deep breath, Jimmy steadied his rifle and returned fire, the recoil jarring through his body. The cacophony of battle surrounded him—the sharp bark of rifles, the distant boom of artillery, the shouted commands and cries of wounded men—all melding into a singular, deafening roar.

Amid the fire fight, Jimmy and his comrades pushed forward, moving in short bursts from one burned out building to the next. The air was acrid. Jimmy's world narrowed to the immediate, the primal instinct to survive driving him onward. His muscles burned, and sweat mingled with the grime on his skin, but he pressed on. As the firefight raged, time lost meaning, and the lines between fear and courage blurred, leaving only the raw, relentless struggle to push the enemy back and to somehow emerge alive.

Jimmy's mind reeled, grief and anger warring within him. The noise of battle receded, leaving only a hollow silence as he crawled toward cover, his heart a heavy, aching weight in his chest. The loss was incomprehensible, a gaping void where Charlie Shea's vibrant presence had once been. Anguish and rage surged through him, and tears blurred his vision as he clutched the dirt, feeling both the fragility and the brutality of life in that singular, devastating moment. Yet, even as the war raged on around him, Jimmy felt a fierce determination ignite within—a promise to carry Charlie's spirit with him, to honor his friend in the only way he knew: by surviving and getting home.

The scene was visceral, a raw and unfiltered testament to the brutality of war. The ground was slick with mud and blood, a gruesome portrait that bore the remnants of shattered lives. Among the chaos, the unmistakable stench of iron hung heavily in the air, mingling with the acrid smell of smoke and cordite. Jimmy's boots slipped in the mud as he moved, each step a reminder of the carnage that surrounded him.

He came across what he thought were Charlie's legs. Nearby, a torn piece of fabric, once part of a uniform, lay half-buried in the muck, stained a deep crimson. Shards of shrapnel glinted dully in the dim light, scattered amidst the remnants of what had once been men, their bravery now reduced to blood and bone. It was a sight that seared itself into his mind, a brutal and haunting image that spoke of sacrifice and loss.

The sight was both terrifying and sobering, a grim reminder of the stakes of their fight. It was a landscape painted in violence, where humanity's basest instincts clashed with its noblest ideals. Jimmy felt the weight of it all pressing down on him, a silent witness to the horrors he wished he could forget. Sadly he knew he never would.

As it was getting dark his platoon decide to make a camp till morning The night was oppressively hot and the darkness thick with death. It was almost tangible. Sgt. Jimmy Donovan lay in a shallow

*"When the patriotic bullshit is all said and done you ask yourself… Do I trust these guys with my life? And in the finale of battle sometimes in the end the answer was no and if the answer was yes… one should be prepared to hold their best friends head in their lap watching them gasp their last breath."*
**US Army Solider, WWII**

foxhole, his breath coming in labored gasps. Around him, the sounds of war persisted—distant artillery, the occasional crack of a rifle, the murmur of men whispering their fears to one another. Jimmy's hands shook, not from the cold, but from the adrenaline that still coursed through his veins. The weight of his rifle felt heavy and the metal cool against his skin.

"I killed a man today," Jimmy said more to himself than anyone else.

In the chaos of battle, there hadn't been time to think, only to react. The enemy soldier had emerged from the smoke, his uniform tattered and his face set in a grim mask. Instinct took over; Jimmy raised his rifle and pulled the trigger. The man dropped, crumpling into the mud, lifeless eyes staring up at the sky. 'There's one 'National Socialist' that'll never see daylight again," Jimmy thought to himself at the time.

He tried to push the image out of his mind, but it lingered haunting him for days. He had trained for these moments, drilled endlessly until his actions were muscle memory. They had told him it was necessary to kill, that it was them or us. But knowing it and feeling it were two different things and actually doing it? Well that was an entirely different matter altogether.

The man he shot had a family, Jimmy thought to himself. Parents, maybe even a wife and kids. He was really no different from Jimmy, just a soldier caught in the maelstrom of a war he didn't start. In another life, they might have shared a beer and swapped stories about their homes and dreams. But here, on this battlefield, at this time, they were enemies. Jimmy understood it in his head but his heart had a bit of a problem with that.

When he was a kid the first time Jimmy Donovan had imagined himself in war, he had envisioned glory. Growing up, he had seen the pictures in newspapers, watched the black-and-white newsreels of soldiers charging valiantly, flags waving behind them. But now, as he crouched in a muddy trench somewhere in Europe, the acrid smell of smoke and the cries of wounded men surrounding him, he realized how naive he had been. The reality of war was not the triumphant adventure he had dreamed of but instead was a relentless, grueling ordeal chipping away at his spirit and at his very soul.

Each day was a blur of chaos and fear, punctuated by the sounds of gunfire and explosions that never seemed to end. The battlefield was a desolate landscape, scarred by craters and strewn with debris, a far cry from the heroic scenes he had once imagined. Jimmy had watched friends fall, their faces frozen in expressions of shock and pain, and had seen villages reduced to ashes, the air heavy with the stench of destruction. As the days dragged on, he felt a growing emptiness within him, a void where his youthful ideals had once thrived. One thing was certain to him especially now... war sure as hell ain't glamorous!

Jimmy's disillusionment deepened with each passing day, and he began to question the purpose of it all. The promises of honor and valor felt hollow against the backdrop of so much senseless loss. Yet, in the midst of his despair, he also discovered an unexpected clarity. He saw the small acts of kindness between soldiers, the shared rations, and the moments of quiet solidarity that spoke of a deeper, more enduring strength. It was in these fleeting glimpses of humanity that Jimmy found a new understanding: the true measure of courage lay not in the glory of battle but in the perseverance to endure and protect the bonds forged in the crucible of war.

Donovan felt a hand on his shoulder and looked up to see Lt. Bud Anderson from Indiana crouching beside him. The Lieutenant's face was weary, eyes shadowed with the same thoughts that plagued Jimmy. Anderson didn't say anything, just squeezed Jimmy's shoulder in silent solidarity. Each man was grappling with his own demons while trying to stay alive.

"You did what ya had to, Jimmy," Anderson finally said, his voice low. "It doesn't get easier, but it's what we're here for. Survive and get back home!"

Survival. The word echoed in Jimmy's head. It was a simple concept, shoot or be shot but the cost was high. He thought of the letter in his pocket, written but never sent. A letter to his parents and Mary, trying to explain why he was here and what he believed he was fighting for. But how could he really put into words the confusion, horror and guilt now inside him?

The night dragged on, the minutes stretching into hours. Jimmy forced himself to focus on the present, on the small tasks that kept him grounded. He made a cup of coffee. Checking his gear and scanning the horizon he kept listening for movement in the darkness. Anything to keep his mind from going back to the lifeless body in the mud he'd caused earlier in the day.

When dawn finally broke, it brought with it a cold, gray light that did little to lift the heaviness in Jimmy's heart or the spirts of those in the foxholes. He rose stiffly, joining the others as they prepared to move out. The day ahead would be filled with more marching, more fighting... more killing.

Jimmy looked at his comrades, seeing the same shadows in their eyes. They were all carrying the weight of their actions. As he shouldered his pack and fell into line, he tried to find some solace in knowing that at least he wasn't alone. They were in this together, and together they would endure. But even as he marched, the ghost of the man he'd killed stayed with him, a reminder of the cost of survival. He couldn't get his face out of his mind.

That night the small campfire cast flickering shadows across the faces of the men, weary and dirt-streaked after another day on the front lines. Donovan sat a little apart from the others, staring into the flames, lost in thought. The weight of recent events pressed heavily on him. He barely noticed when Lt. Anderson approached and sat down beside him.

"Mind if I join you?" Anderson asked, breaking the silence and sitting down.

Jimmy shook his head, his eyes still fixed on the fire. "No, sir. It's your campfire too."

For a few moments, neither spoke. The crackle of the fire and the distant sounds of war were the only interruptions. Anderson finally broke the silence. "You did really well out there today, Jimmy. The men look up to you and you're a natural leader."

Jimmy's jaw tightened. "Did I? I killed a man today, Lieutenant. Shot him right in the head. He couldn't have been more than my age."

Anderson sighed, his gaze thoughtful. "I know. It's never really easy, is it? Glad he didn't shoot you!"

Jimmy turned to face him, his eyes haunted. "How do you do it, sir? How do you deal with it? The killing, I mean. I keep seeing his face when I close my eyes. I can't get any damn sleep!"

Anderson leaned forward, resting his elbows on his knees. "It never gets easier, Jimmy. Not if you're human. But we're here for a reason. We're here to stop something much bigger and much worse than the individual lives we take. It's hard to see in the heat of the moment, but every man we kill means fewer who will hurt the innocent, fewer who'll carry out the orders of that goddamn madman."

Jimmy shook his head. "I know that, sir. But knowing it doesn't make it any easier. I keep thinking about his family. Someone's going to get a damn letter that their boy isn't coming home."

Anderson nodded. "And what about our families, Jimmy? Every time we fight, we protect them. Every enemy soldier we stop means one less who might kill our brothers, our friends and maybe our own children someday. And left unchecked I believe that is what the Nazi intend to do!"

Jimmy ran a hand through his hair, frustration and sorrow mingling in his eyes. "I get it. I do. But it's just... how do you make peace with it? How do you live with yourself afterward?"

The Lieutenant's eyes softened. "You never make peace with it, Jimmy. You just carry it, like a scar. It's a part of who you are now. You remind yourself of why you're here, and you lean on your comrades. Talk to them. Talk to me. We're all in this together. Besides when one of your best friends is laying there with his belly hanging out

70

because of what a Nazi did... you'll know exactly what to do!" he said.

Jimmy nodded slowly, the words sinking in. "Thanks, Lieutenant. I guess I needed to hear that. No worry... I'll always do my duty," he said.

Anderson smiled, a weary but genuine expression. "Anytime, Jimmy. I know you will. And just remember, it's okay to feel guilty. It means you still have a conscience. It means you're still human. Just don't let it paralyze you. We need you out there. The men need you and I need you."

Jimmy looked back at the fire, its warmth and light a small comfort. "I won't forget that, sir. Thanks."

As Anderson stood to leave, he placed a hand on Jimmy's shoulder, a gesture of camaraderie and support. "Get some rest, Sergeant. We've got a long day ahead of us."

Jimmy watched him walk away, feeling a little lighter, though the weight of his actions would never fully lift. He took a deep breath, letting the night air fill his lungs, and whispered to the flickering flames, "One step towards home..."

In the dim glow of a single candle, Jimmy sat hunched over his tiny makeshift writing desk, the edges of his uniform fraying from constant wear. The war had turned the European landscape into a backdrop of relentless hardship and peril, but in this small corner of his temporary quarters, Jimmy found some peace. Before him lay a blank sheet of paper, a canvas for the words that would bridge the chasm between the battlefield and Ohio.

Each letter he received from home was a lifeline, a precious connection to the world he had left behind. The inked words of his mother's careful handwriting carried the warmth of her kitchen, the scent of her baked pies, and the familiar cadence of her voice. These letters were more than just updates from home; they were tokens of love, fragments of normalcy in a world turned upside down by war. Dad didn't write, it was not his nature, but Jimmy knew his thoughts were with and for his son.

For soldiers on the front lines, mail call is a sacred ritual. The arrival of the mail truck stirred more excitement than any military parade. Men gathered, faces alight with anticipation, each one hoping to hear their name called out. A letter from home meant that someone cared, that their sacrifices were noticed and appreciated. It was a reminder that beyond the barbed wire and muddy trenches, life continued and they had something back home worth fighting for.

Jimmy's letters to and from his family were important. He poured his heart into every line, crafting stories of camaraderie and small victories, and sparing them the gruesome details of battle.

He wanted his mother to picture him as strong and unbroken, a far cry from the reality that were his days and nights. Each letter he sent was a piece of himself, an assurance that he was still alive and still the son she remembered.

On days when the gunfire was relentless and the sky was dark with smoke, Jimmy would reach into his jacket and pull out a letter from his sweetheart, Mary. Her words wrapped around him like a protective shield, her promises of a future together fueling his resolve. The scent of her perfume lingered on paper, a whisper of love that defied the scent and noise of war.

The importance of these letters transcends their physical form. They're beacons of hope, anchors of sanity, and symbols of sheer stubbornness. For Jimmy and countless others, they provided a mental escape, a way to momentarily transcend the horrors surrounding them. The letters were proof that soldiers were remembered and loved.

In the vast impersonal machinery of war, letters and mail were the most personal of treasures. They were reminders that, despite the distance and danger, the hearts at home beat in time with those on the front lines. In every fold of the paper, in every stroke of the pen, lay a promise of return, of peace, and of the life he left that seemed to wait just beyond the horizon.

Donovan was now a seasoned soldier, hardened by three years of warfare over France, Belgium and Italy. The Army recognized him for his cool head under fire and his unflinching loyalty to his teammates. The mission to disrupt the German rail lines was one of the most risky jobs he had ever undertaken, but Donovan recognized its necessity and importance. Disrupting the enemy's supplies would offer the Allies a critical advantage.

For his next assignment James got orders to destroy a train load of Nazi military supplies heading for an isolated German outpost. The train was a long, serpentine beast that would twist its way through the Alps. Each curve and turn brought with it an ominous moan of metal under strain as the German train wound its way through the Italian

countryside. His orders were clear... make sure that the train shipment did not reach its destination in one piece. It was actually a mundane task, one that needed little more than his presence and a match to light the dynamite. It was a typical job, but at least he got to blow stuff up so he was happy about that.

The German rail station shone softly in the moonlight as he crouching down in the underbrush and gazing through the rifle scope. The shadows at the station moved with an eerie precision. It was a straightforward operation for Jimmy; gain intelligence beyond enemy lines undetected and then return without being discovered. That was the plan. However, conflicts have a way of making even the best plans more difficult and sometimes damn near impossible to execute. 'Do or Die'.

As Donovan's platoon marched across the Italian countryside, local resistance fighters joined them. This movement took place under the cover of darkness and they were successful in reaching their aim; a rail yard that was tucked away in a tiny town. In the yard, a convoy of trains, including many brand-new 'Kullwagen' refrigerated railway boxcars. They were getting ready to depart.

Jimmy's goal was direct... produce as much turmoil as possible by planting explosives on the rails, derailing the trains, and causing as much disruption to Nazi supply operations as possible. When the unit got back from planting the explosives, the CO assigned Donovan and Private Jack Harris with the responsibility of hunting for enemy patrols in the surrounding region. There was a palpable sense of unease in the atmosphere, and every stir in the woods sounded like danger. The two young soldiers slipped cautiously between the shadows, constantly on high alert for any sign of impending danger, training their eyes and ears to detect the tiniest sign of the enemy.

Jimmy made adjustments to the volume of his walkie talkie as he was experiencing radio static.

"Alpha to Omega, come in, Omega."

In response, the voice of Lieutenant Daniels crackled. "This is Omega. What's your current standing, Alpha, over…?

Jimmy hurriedly checked the terminal. "Everything fine. Awaiting instruction. Over!"

"Proceed to the selected rendezvous and report anything you find," advised Daniels. "And for Christ's sake keep your head down!"

"Roger that Alpha… Out!" came Jimmy's response.

Concealing himself in the darkness and slinging his rifle over his shoulder, Jimmy disappeared into the darkness only his breath visible in the chilly night air. The crunch of melting snow underfoot served as a stark reminder of the severe winter that Europe has been experiencing the worse in the past century. As he got closer to the forest's edge, he stopped and listened. A train's distant hum sounded throughout the valley so he knew that he was in the right place… now if he could just find the train.

As he crept closer his senses became more acute. The security at the station was minimal, with only a few sentries patrolling the perimeter of the facility. After patiently waiting for the right moment, Jimmy sneaked past the security guards to make his way to the freight yard. When he looked ahead, he saw a line of almost new train cars that were loaded with supplies headed to the German front lines.

But calamity was lurking just around the corner at that precise moment. The charges were placed and the group was getting ready to withdraw then unexpectedly, a German patrol that was significantly larger than expected came across the sabotaging operation. An explosion of gunfire shattered the tranquility of the night. While standing right next to Donovan, Harris was shot in the head and passed away instantly. In the ensuing chaos, the American team scattered, each man fighting to stay alive and complete the mission.

By the next day the sun had barely risen when more shots rang out, shattering the early morning stillness. Donovan hit the dirt, the sharp crack of rifle fire echoing through the forest. He scrambled behind a fallen log, heart pounding, as bullets whizzed past him, tearing through the leaves and kicking up dirt.

"Incoming!" someone shouted, and a mortar shell exploded nearby, the blast wave slamming Jimmy into the ground. His ears rang, but he forced himself to focus, peeking over the log to assess the situation. A squad of German soldiers had ambushed them, their dark uniforms blending with the shadows of the trees.

Jimmy clutched his M1, feeling the reassuring weight of the rifle. He took a deep breath, aimed, and squeezed the trigger. The rifle bucked against his shoulder, and he saw one of the enemy soldiers drop. The familiar ping of the empty clip signaled him to reload. He pulled another eight-round clip from his belt, thumbed it into the rifle, and resumed firing.

"Flank left!" Lt. Anderson's voice cut through the chaos. Jimmy nodded, signaling to two other soldiers to follow. They darted through the trees, keeping low, the ground trembling with each explosion and smoke hiding their position.

The battlefield was a nightmarish scene of devastation and chaos, where the line between life and death blurred in an instant. As the smoke cleared from the latest barrage, Jimmy found himself frozen in shock, his mind struggling to process the grisly reality before him. His comrade, once full of life and laughter, lay lifeless beside him, his head gruesomely severed by the brutal force of the explosion. The sight was both surreal and horrifying, a jarring reminder of war's indiscriminate cruelty.

Jimmy's breath caught in his throat as he stared at the gruesome tableau, his heart pounding in his chest. The ground beneath him felt unsteady, the world tilting dangerously as he fought to comprehend the loss. The blood-soaked earth seemed to swallow all sound, leaving only a deafening silence in its wake. He could not tear his eyes away from his friend, the bond they shared now severed in a violent and irreversible way.

A wave of nausea and grief washed over him, threatening to overwhelm his senses. He went behind a tree and threw up. Yet, amidst the horror, as he righted himself, a grim determination took root. The brutal image seared into his mind became a driving force, fueling his resolve to survive and honor his fallen brother. In the heart of war's grotesque reality, Jimmy found a reason to keep moving forward, to fight not just to win, but for the memory of those who had paid the ultimate price.

Suddenly Jimmy heard the distinctive rattle of a German MG42 machine gun, its rapid fire slicing through the air. He dropped to one knee, bringing Peggy to his shoulder and firing at the muzzle flashes in the distance. The MG42 was a deadly weapon, its high rate of fire was capable of cutting down men in seconds. Jimmy's rounds found their mark, and then the machine gun fell silent.

Beside him, Harris' body lay there and Jimmy got mad. The crack of the carbine was sharper, its rounds flying towards the enemy with more precision. And Jimmy could be heard muttering a steady stream of curses and prayers.

A German soldier appeared from behind a tree, his Mauser Karabiner 98k raised. Jimmy reacted instantly, firing his Garand. The German soldier crumpled, his rifle clattering to the ground. Jimmy's hands shook as he reloaded, the reality of the kill hitting him even in the heat of battle.

"Keep moving!" Anderson yelled, and Jimmy pushed forward, ducking as another mortar shell exploded nearby. The ground shook, sending dirt and debris into the air. He could feel the heat of the explosion and the shockwave rattling his bones.

Suddenly, a hand grenade landed a few feet away. Jimmy's eyes widened in horror. "Grenade!" he shouted, diving behind a tree. The grenade exploded, the blast wave sending shards of wood and metal in all directions. Jimmy felt a sharp pain in his leg, but he forced himself to ignore it, adrenaline pushing him onward.

They reached a small clearing, where the Germans had set up a makeshift command post. Jimmy could see their officer shouting orders, his voice barely audible over the din of battle. Without hesitation, Jimmy aimed his rifle and fired, the officer's body jerking as the bullets found their target. It's really the first time he'd killed for sure.

With their leader down, the remaining Nazi soldiers faltered. Jimmy's squad pressed the advantage, firing with grim determination. A grenade was lobbed into the center of the enemy position, the explosion sending bodies and equipment flying. The surviving Germans retreated, their morale broken.

As the enemy fled, Jimmy collapsed against a tree, breathing heavily. The forest was eerily quiet now, the sounds of battle replaced by the groans of the wounded and the crackling of small fires. He glanced down at his leg, where a piece of shrapnel had torn through his pants and lodged in his flesh. The pain was starting to break through the haze of adrenaline, but he knew it could've been worse.

The Lieutenant knelt beside him, his face pale and streaked with sweat. "You okay, Jimmy?"

Jimmy nodded, wincing as he shifted his weight. "I'll live. How about you?"

"Still in one piece," Anderson said, managing a shaky smile. "We did it!"

Jimmy looked around at his comrades, some tending to the wounded, others securing the area. They had survived another battle, but the war was far from over. He felt a mix of relief and exhaustion, the weight of their mission pressing down on him even harder."Good work, everyone," Lt. Anderson called out, his voice carrying a note of pride. "We held our ground. Get those wounds tended to and regroup."

As the men got ready to move out, Jimmy allowed himself a moment to breathe. The fighting had been fierce, but they had come through it in one piece together. And in the midst of the fire and chaos, he had found a strength he hadn't known he possessed. The war would continue, as would he.

But when the smoke cleared Donovan suddenly found himself cut off from the rest of his unit. With German soldiers closing in, he had no choice but to seek refuge anywhere he could find it. Jimmy's breath caught in his throat. The intel suggested these boxcars held something valuable to the German war effort. He had to get inside.

His heart pounded as he reached the first rail car. It was locked. Second one? Locked. The third one had a closed door but he tried it and it slid open. He climbed up, careful to stay out of sight, and peered inside. Empty. He moved to the next car, and the next, finding them filled with crates and barrels. Finally, he reached the end of the row. The last cars were different—they were the new refrigerated rail cars but all the steel doors were closed tight. Spotting an open door lock, he tried it and it slid open. He ducked inside, hoping to evade capture until the Nazi patrol moved on.

The rhythmic clattering of steel wheels against iron tracks had always been a kind of lullaby to Donovan. As a solider he'd ridden innumerable trains throughout the world, the repetitive sound a constant companion during extended deployments. But this train journey, in the bitter European winter of 1944, just may prove to be his last.

# CHAPTER 5

## All Aboard!
### The Railways of a Fallen Empire

*"At Least Mussolini made the trains run on time!"*
Old Italian Saying.

As the sun rose above the picturesque Apennine Mountains, it produced lengthy shadows across the rural area of Italy. Battles had scarred the area, and centuries of struggle and occupation had worn down the people who lived there. One of the most powerful empires in history, the Italian Empire was falling apart, with its infrastructure in ruins and its administration in turmoil. But even in the middle of the mayhem, there was one item that was a constant and did not change: the Trains. The railway network in Italy spans a total distance of about 25000 kilometers (1600 miles), which makes it an essential component of the country's infrastructure. Before air, rail was the only way.

Throughout the decades, Italy's rail network had served as the nation's vital support system, linking the country's cities, towns, and villages through a complex network of iron and steel railroads. During WWII, the trains had transported soldiers to the front lines, supplies to the cities that were under siege, and refugees to safe havens. During this time, the railways were both an essential asset and a strategic objective for the Allies as they

advanced toward Nazi Germany. Jimmy loved rail travel and had thought about staying in Europe and traveling around after the war but then after he thought about it he realized that there wouldn't be very much left to see.

The advance of the Allied forces was unrelenting. The British and American soldiers, with the help of local partisan fighters, marched through the Italian Peninsula with a grim resolve. The strain caused the Axis powers to retreat, eventually breaking down their lines. Rome, Florence, and Bologna were just a few of the towns that were constantly being bombarded and assaulted. The bombs dropped with a horrifying regularity, reducing historic structures to rubble and transforming avenues that were once buzzing with activity into streets of desolation.

While all of this was going on, Signore Giovanni Moretti was standing on the platform of a little train station near Emilia-Romagna. The station was of simple construction with a roof made of cracked and worn red clay tiles, and the walls covered with faded posters and graffiti. Giovanni, a middle-aged guy with a large physique and a face that showed signs of aging, wore the uniform of a train conductor and had a face that had seen several years of wear and tear. He had spent most of his life on these tracks but had witnessed nothing quite like the turmoil that had been occurring over the previous year or two. He hated the Nazis and the Fascists and thought both were equally bad.

The Allies had been seen in the area obviously advanced recon platoons gathering intel before an invasion. Giovanni sat on an old wooden char tipped back on its hind legs and staining under his weight as he watched the sun go down behind the Italian mountains in the distance.

"Psssst hey Paisan!" came a whispered voice from behind some freight and boxes. "Don't say anything and don't look!" said the voice of paratrooper Jimmy Donovan, "Are the... are the krauts nearby? Just nod..." Yes came the answer. "Motion toward which direction" Giovanni motioned towards the east. "Tap your foot for how many... one stomp equals 10 soldiers," Donovan said. The foot, size 12, tapped 3 times... 30 men. "Graze Senior!" he said as he started to sneak off deeper into the near-by brush.

"Wait Sir..." said Giovanni. He looked around got up and stealthily followed Donovan into the bushes. In broken English the Italian conductor needed some intel of his own,

"When are you comin? Things is bad and we can't hold out much longer. The partisans are behind you and they do sabotage as much as they dare to without getting shot!" Giovanni explained.

"That's A-OK you're my Paisan... you tell 'em to keep it up and we'll be here by next week!" Donovan said. "The main thing is don't let the damn Nazi's blow this station up, OK? Si?"

"Si sir!" came the response.

They sat behind the bushes for 20-30 minutes trading news and catching up. Donavan shared news about the invasion and how Italy was about

to fall while Giovanni talked about the brutal occupation by the German and where their heavy artillery and tanks were located. He also told Donovan about the new refrigerated rail cars and the vital shipment about to go out. Perhaps most importantly he talked Donovan thru the tricky lock system for accessing the box cars. Finally Donovan got up, picked up his rifle, said "Grazi Giovanni… Be seeing you again soon!" as he moved off into the darkness. Both men were longing for the day when then could sit and talk in freedom without the fear of getting shot. And little did Donovan know that he would travel to this very station again in the near future.

In the morning the station, saw a lot of activity. Nazi soldiers and local civilians filled the station, their faces expressing a mixture of fear and exhaustion. The wheels of the trains screeched as they rumbled in and out of the station on the iron rails. The air was filled with the strong odor of coal and steam, mixed with the pungent odor of burning buildings seen in the distance.

Giovanni's look swept over the gathering, looking for well-known individuals to recognize. Young troops were attempting to hide their terror with bravado, and he observed moms clinging to their children. He also noticed elderly men with eyes that seemed to be haunted. Every single one of them was heavily reliant on the trains, on the railways that had once been Italy's national pride. The war had altered everything.

Amidst the noise, a voice shouted, "CIAO Gio?!!"

When he spun around, Paolo, his oldest friend and fellow Conductor, was standing there. These days Paolo's sparkling eyes were sometimes obscured by concern, despite the fact that he was a hefty guy with a thick mustache, wire rim glasses and a perpetual twinkle in his eye. He was a funny man.

"Paolo," Giovanni responded as he embraced his trusted companion. "How are things goin in the northern region?"

Paolo shook his head. "It's no good. Despite withdrawing, the Nazis are leaving nothing and there's lots of damage. Every single object, including bridges, railroads, and stations, is being destroyed," he said. "The Allies are attempting to maintain open lines of communication, but it's a never-ending battle," Paolo continued.

Giovanni gave a brief nod. He was familiar with the accounts, and he had witnessed some of the destruction with his own eyes. Constant assaults were being launched on the rails, which were being attacked by both the fleeing Germans and the advancing Allies. The retreating Germans blasted several stations, destroyed bridges and ripped up tracks. However, despite the damage, the trains somehow continued to operate. They had no choice but to continue running. After all there were schedules to keep.

"Any new info from Rome?" Giovanni inquired.

Paolo stated that, according to the information he had, the city is still refusing to give in. "But it's only a matter of time. The Allies are pushing hard, and the Germans are running away like scared little girls!" he said as he pranced on the platform like some sort of little ballerina. Then he suddenly got very serious, "At a moment's notice, we need to be prepared to move quickly in any direction... and that's no joke!"

Giorgio let out a loud sigh. Maria, his wife, and their two children and almost all the members of his family lived in or near Rome. It had been months since he'd last seen them, and the feelings of uneasiness were consuming him. Every day, he worried about their well-being and prayed for their safety from the atrocities of war.

Paolo placed a reassuring hand on Giovanni's shoulder, as if he could somehow sense what Giovanni was thinking. "My friend, we'll prevail over this. One of our greatest strengths has always been the trains. At any cost, we'll ensure they continue to function, no matter what," he said.

Forcing a smile, Giovanni said. "I hope you're right, Paolo, I hope you're right. Our job is to keep them operational. We will!" He went on to share information on his meeting the American solider in the bushes and that the 'Yanks are in their way!'

Giovanni often found himself shaking his head in amusement at his friend Paolo's antics. Paolo was a wiry man with a perpetual grin and a knack for finding humor in the most unlikely situations, a gift that was rare and precious amid the chaos of WWII. They worked together on the Italian railway, their days spent repairing tracks and transporting supplies, a task made bearable by Paolo's endless supply of jokes and stories. It seemed Paolo could make even the sternest Nazi officer crack a smile, his laughter was infectious and unwavering despite the grim reality.

One afternoon, as the sun beat down mercilessly on the tracks, Paolo concocted a plan to lighten the mood. "Giovanni, my friend," he said with a wink, "I've discovered a new way to speed up our work." Giovanni watched skeptically as Paolo disappeared into the small shed near the station. Moments later, he emerged wearing an oversized conductor's cap and holding a makeshift baton fashioned from a broken broomstick. With exaggerated precision, he began directing the imaginary orchestra of workers, each movement absurdly theatrical.

The other workers stopped to watch, their exhaustion momentarily forgotten as they chuckled at Paolo's impromptu performance. He pranced and twirled along the tracks, conducting with wild abandon, his antics drawing laughter and applause from the men. Even Giovanni, usually the more reserved of the pair, found himself joining in, mimicking Paolo's exaggerated gestures. For a few precious minutes, the war was forgotten, replaced by Paolo's gift of laughter, a reminder that even in the darkest of times, joy can still be found.

The fall of Rome was fast and violent. The Eternal City, with its ancient monuments and majestic architecture, had stood as a symbol of power and civilization for millennia. But by the spring of 1944, however, it had turned into a battleground and was a city that was under siege.

The massive offensive known as Operation Diadem had been initiated by the Allies with the objective of penetrating the German defensive lines and seizing their capital city of Rome. The fighting was intense, and there were a lot of casualties. Over many weeks, the city was bombarded from both air and ground shelling. Buildings collapsed, fires were raging, and the streets were crowded with people who were fleeing, injured or in the process of dying.

Because of his determination to locate his family, Giovanni had been successful in making his way to Rome. He arrived in the city amidst the chaos, the train station a scene of utter pandemonium. People were running everywhere, desperate to escape the

fighting, to find shelter from the bombs.

He pushed his way through the crowd, his heart pounding in his chest. He had to find Maria and the children. He had to know they were safe.

"Maria!" he yelled out, his voice scarcely heard over the racket. "Maria!"

He searched the station, the streets, the shelters for hours and then days. Everywhere he looked, he saw despair. But there was no sign of his family.

Days turned into weeks. The fighting intensified, the city teetering on the brink of collapse. Giovanni continued his search, his hope dwindling with each passing day. He found himself drawn to the railways, to the tracks that had been his life's work. Somehow he knew that this is where she

95

would be. The trains still ran, though sporadically, carrying supplies and refugees. In a city on the edge of oblivion, the trains were a true lifeline and the train station was the hub of the community.

One evening he was standing on the platform of a rail station that had been bombed out when he heard a voice coming from behind him.

"Giovanni?!" The young woman said in shock.

He turned to find a young woman standing there; her face pallid and haggard, her clothes ragged and soiled. It took him a moment to recognize her.

"Maria? Oh my God...Maria?!" he called out.

She nodded, tears now streaming down her face. "Giovanni, thank God I found you. I thought I'd never see you again. Thank God!"

They embraced, holding each other tightly for several minutes. Giovanni's eyes filled with tears as he looked at his wife, his heart breaking at her suffering.

"Where are the children?" he questioned, his voice cracking. Not a day had gone by without Giovanni thinking about his wife and kids. It was an all consuming need to find his family, alive or dead.

"They're safe," Maria said. "They're in the countryside with my sister. It was necessary for us to leave the city. It was just too dangerous!"

Giovanni gave a slight nod, a sense of relief washing over him. "Thank God. I was so worried."

"Not to worry... we're safe now," Maria said, her voice firm. "But we do need to get out of here. This city is falling apart!"

Giovanni looked around, the devastation all too clear. "The trains," he said. "We can still use the trains. And we need to hurry, the America said they would be here in days!"

Maria gave a nod. "OK. We can stay with my sister if we can get to the countryside. It's safer."

The Allies were coming and the Nazis had made it clear that they would destroy everything rather than leave it for the Americans and British. Giovanni took her hand, determination in his eyes. "Don't worry my love, we'll make it. My trains will bring us there."

The voyage was risky. The railways, long a symbol of Italy's power and unity, were now a target. Bridges were blown up, railroads ripped apart, stations blasted into ruin. Despite the wreckage, the trains continued to criss-cross the country.

Giovanni and Maria made their way through the ruined city, avoiding the bombed-out buildings and streets filled with dead as the constant sound and threat of gunfire filled the air. They found a train heading north, its destination uncertain. They didn't care. The conductor, a weary man with a haunting look in his eyes, let them aboard without question and without a ticket. There were no tickets, no schedules, only the strong urge to flee.

Families, Italian soldiers, elderly people, and young people were among the refugees who were packed onto the train. Every one of them was huddled together, and the expressions on their faces were identical: a mixture of fear and hope. Giovanni and Maria found a spot near the back of the train car and sat down.

As the train rumbled along the tracks, Giovanni's mind drifted to the past. He recalled the times before the war, when the railways had been a source of pride and advancement for the communities that they served. His first month as a Conductor was uneventful, he recalled the joy of going across the country and connecting people and places. He also recalled the enthusiasm of his first day. The railways had been his passion since boyhood and now they were his salvation.

The train traveled through the night, its path marked by the distant sounds of explosions and the eerie glow of fires on the far horizon. At each stop, more individuals got on, their desperation evident. Giovanni did his best to help, offering what little comfort and knowledge he could.

"Where we goin?" Maria asked with a whisper.

"North," Giovanni replied. "It's safer there. Maybe we can make it to the Swiss boarder."

Maria nodded, her eyes displaying a mixture of relief and concern. "As long as we're together that's all I really care about now," she added.

The train resumed its trip, traveling past cities and villages that had been reduced to ruins. The railways were a lifeline, a frail thread uniting the ruins of a once-great nation. Giovanni could see the strain on the faces of the railway workers, the constant fear of sabotage and attack. But they kept going, driven by a sense of duty and determination.

As the train continued on it was coming upon Giovanni's old home town. Nestled in a lush valley surrounded by rolling hills and olive groves, the Italian village of San Pietro had long been his haven of peace and beauty. He fondly remembered its cobblestone streets winding gently through clusters of red terracotta-roofed houses, each adorned with window boxes overflowing with vibrant geraniums. The scent of freshly baked bread and blooming jasmine filled the air, mingling with the laughter of children playing in the village square. At the heart of the village stood an ancient stone church, its bell tower rising proudly above the rooftops, a symbol of the community's spirit. Giovanni had rung that bell many times as a boy.

But like everywhere in Europe as the war crept closer, San Pietro's tranquility was shattered. The distant rumble of artillery grew louder with each passing day, and soon the once-peaceful valley echoed with the sounds of conflict. The sky, once a canvas of serene blues, was now streaked with the dark trails of fighter planes. Residents sought shelter in their cellars, clutching cherished memories and whispering prayers as the village they loved was caught in the crossfire. Explosions tore through the cobblestones, sending clouds of dust and debris into the air, and the vibrant homes that had stood for generations crumbled under the relentless assault.

When the dust finally settled, San Pietro was a shadow of its former self. As the train slowly passed the town Giovanni and Maria sat in stunned silence looking out the window at the ruins.

The village square, once alive with chatter and song, lay silent and desolate. The church bell, now fallen and cracked, lay amidst the ruins in silence. The school and train station were now bombed out hulks. Yet, amid the devastation, the villagers slowly emerged, their faces etched with sorrow but also with determination. They gathered in the ruins, beginning the slow, painful task of rebuilding, their resilience a testament to the enduring spirit of San Pietro. Despite the destruction, Giovanni could see that the soul of the village remained unbroken. The train continued on

That afternoon, as the train approached a bridge, the conductor announced that they would have to stop. The bridge had sustained damage, and repairs were currently being carried out. Giovanni and Maria joined the other passengers as they disembarked, waiting anxiously by the tracks.

Giovanni watched as the railway workers toiled to repair the bridge, their efforts a testament to their resilience. He felt a surge of pride and gratitude. The railways had always been more than just a means of transportation.

During World War II, Italy's railroad system was a central component of the country's infrastructure, playing a significant role in both civilian life and military operations. The state-owned Ferrovie Dello Stato (FS) operated most of the rail network, which was extensive and well-developed. Before the war, Italy had constructed an enormous and relatively modern rail network, with important lines linking significant towns and regions. The network contained both standard gauge and narrow gauge rail lines, allowing transit and transport across the country. It was possible to make connections between Milan and Rome, Venice and Naples, and other major urban centers through the use of major routes. Additionally, the rail lines extended to smaller towns and rural areas, completing the network in its entirety from Florence and Genoa in the north to Naples and Sicily to the south.

Electricity was introduced into certain sections of the rail network by the 1930s, particularly in the central and northern regions, resulting in an increase in both efficiency and dependability. Italy had made investments in modern infrastructure, which ultimately resulted in the country's rail transportation system being one of best in Europe.

As the war wore on the rail system became increasingly important for the movement of troops, military equipment, and supplies as the war moved forward. When it came to transporting soldiers to various fronts, the Italian army placed a significant amount of reliance on the rail network. This was true not just inside Italy but also throughout its possessions in North Africa and the Balkans. Because of military goals and ongoing hostilities, passengers frequently overcrowded trains, and it became challenging to predict their timetables. The rail network's strategic importance made it a key target for Allied bombs and sabotage by resistance fighters. To disrupt Nazi supply lines and military operations, resistance fighters frequently targeted key junctions and train stations.

The impact of Allied bombings caused much destruction with extensive damage to Italy's rail infrastructure. Bridges were destroyed, tracks were bombed, and stations were reduced to rubble. Cities like Milan, Turin, and Naples, which were key rail hubs, experienced severe destruction. Despite the constant attacks, Italian railway workers, often under duress, worked tirelessly to repair damaged tracks and restore service. In addition, the German military, which had taken control of a significant portion of Italy's rail network after 1943, the Italians made significant efforts to repair the lines in order to ensure that they continued to function.

With the German occupation and control of Italy following the armistice in 1943, the Wehrmacht extensively used the country's railways. The German forces prioritized the rail network for their military logistics, often at the expense of civilian needs. However, Italian partisans sabotaged the railways, successfully attacking trains and rail facilities. The aim was to disrupt German supply lines and hurt military operations. They did.

Post-War recovery and reconstruction was long in coming. After the war, the rail network was in a total state of disrepair. With the help of the 'Marshall Plan', the Italian government embarked on extensive efforts to reconstruct and update the rail system. The wartime use and subsequent destruction of Italy's railways left a lasting impact on the country. The rail system's role during the war highlighted its strategic importance and set the stage for post-war modernization.

Italy's railroad system during World War II was a vital but beleaguered asset. It facilitated the movement of troops and supplies, supported civilian travel, and played a key role in the broader conflict. However, it also faced relentless attacks, both from Allied bombings and from partisan sabotage, leading to significant challenges in maintaining and operating the network.

The end of the war marked the beginning of a lengthy and laborious process of rebuilding and modernizing the railways, which laid the groundwork for the contemporary rail network Italy enjoys today.

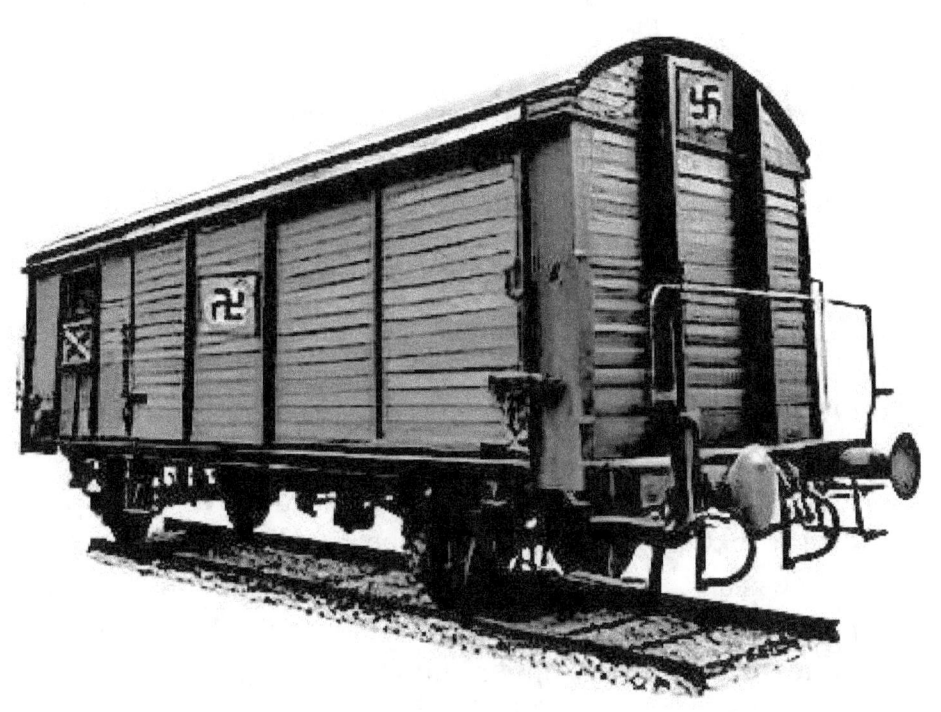

# CHAPTER 6

## Wartime Innovation
### *The New Kühlwagen Fridge Car*

*"An Army runs on its stomach!"*
Gen. George S Patton

Between the cold expanses of the Eastern Front and the scorched sand dunes of North Africa, the German war machine was in full motion during the closing months of 1943. Its grip extended from the Eastern Front near Russia to Morocco and North Africa. A more subdued revolution was taking place on the railways of Europe at the same time that the chaos and carnage was taking place.

Despite the terrible circumstances of the war, the 'Wehrmacht' (the German Army) had adopted a new form of refrigeration rail car aimed at insuring their troops got what they needed nutritionally.

"Kullwagen" was the name given to the sleek, steel leviathans that were the new German Refrigeration railway cars. These boxcars were a wonder of technical technology. They kept the temperature constant while transporting valuable cargo like as meat, dairy products, and vegetables, necessary for the Wehrmacht to sustain its operations. Both the supply lines and the front lines were getting longer and more dangerous with each passing day. The front lines were located a great distance from the fertile fields of Germany. The idea was not new. As early as the turn of the century, people used "Ice Cars" to transport food in the American west. They placed the food in insulated boxcars with enormous volumes of ice. However, this was the first time mechanical refrigeration was utilized.

Now the Nazi's were evil of that there can be no doubt, but at the same time one can somewhat admire their innovation and efficiency. Nazi Captain Friedrich Muller, a careful commander with a remarkable eye for detail, was the one who was at the heart of this logistical dance. Muller had the responsibility of coordinating the delivery of supplies to the Eastern Front. He was well aware of the significance of his mission; the morale and efficiency of the troops depended on the provision of attractive meals that are high in nutrients. Troops who are starving tend to lose their morale, and during the harsh winters in Russia, food was just as much of a weapon as bullets or explosives.

Muller coordinated a complicated schedule to make sure they loaded the Kühlwagen's as quickly as possible and sent them out with military precision. The trains moved in a continuous loop, transporting fresh produce to the East and returning to the West with the spoils of war. This loot composed piles of goods and foodstuffs that had been confiscated from the territories under Nazi occupation.

As the German soldiers on the Eastern Front awaited the supply trains, they did so with a mixture of eagerness and despair. The terrain had

been transformed into a frozen hellscape because of the hard winter. The cold and snow that covered the trenches ate away at their bones, causing them to lose their strength and their willpower. When the Kühlwagen box cars arrived, it was a momentary reprieve from the never-ending fight.

As the trains neared the front lines, a frenzy of action greeted them, and people welcomed them with open arms. Although exhaustion lined their faces, the promise of a hot meal lit up their expressions as they efficiently unloaded the precious cargo. The sight of fresh vegetables, slabs of beef, and even the occasional luxury such as butter or chocolate, soothing for battered spirits.

A young German infantryman named Hans Becker from Heidelberg kept watch as the supplies were being distributed to the various locations. Even amid the conflict, the refrigeration cars could keep food fresh, which left him in awe of their ingenuity. Hans had spent his childhood on a farm in Bavaria, and the Kühlwagen brought back memories of his childhood home and, more importantly, of simpler times before the world was consumed by hate and flames.

However, the Kühlwagen, just like any other innovation or weapon of war, came with a price tag. Because of the German army's reliance on these trains, the rail network was subjected to a significant amount of pressure. Partisan attacks,

Allied bombardment, and the sheer logistical impossibility of maintaining the lines meant that every trip was fraught with risk. Losing a single train could mean the difference between life and death for thousands of Nazi soldiers.

Muller was acutely aware of the dangers present. Due to his tireless efforts, Muller frequently sacrificed sleep to guarantee that the supply lines ran uninterrupted. When he became obsessed with the Kühlwagen, the smooth, icy surfaces of the vehicle became a reflection of his own unyielding determination. He realized the success of the German army was contingent not only on these trains but also, by extension, directly upon him.

During a harsh winter night, when the temperature was dropping and snow falling relentlessly, Muller received word that a partisan attack was coming. The supply train traversed a region that was well known for guerrilla activity. Traveling to Stalingrad, the train carried fresh provisions as well as troops to guard it, Muller's pulse pounded as he issued orders organizing a contingent to guard the train line.

Nazi Lieutenant Karl Fischer, stationed at the front lines of Stalingrad, was among the first to receive the supplies. Fischer had witnessed firsthand the toll that starvation and malnutrition took on his men. They were a determined group, but the brutal cold and lack of food sapped their spirit to fight.

As the Kühlwagen were unloaded, Fischer witnessed a remarkable shift in his soldiers. The sight of fresh meat, crisp vegetables, and dairy products was almost surreal. The soldiers worked

with a renewed energy, their gaunt faces breaking into smiles as they prepared their first hot, nutritious meal in weeks. For a moment, the horrors of war seemed to recede, replaced by the simple joy of shared sustenance.

Müller and his team stayed in Stalingrad for a few days, overseeing the distribution of the supplies and ensuring that the Kühlwagen were properly maintained for the return journey. Müller maintained extensive notes, writing reports for the High Command on the functioning of the refrigerated cars and their influence on soldier attitudes and efficiency.

The victory of the Kühlwagen at Stalingrad was a turning point. The military promptly placed orders for additional units, and soon, refrigerated rail trains became a familiar sight on the supply lines traveling to various fronts. They delivered everything from fresh vegetables to medical supplies, ensuring that the German army could retain its operational capabilities.

To gain a better understanding of how the Kühlwagen was performing in real-world conditions, Weiss made multiple trips to the front lines and met with both soldiers and commanders. During his conversation, he met with individuals such as Fischer, who lauded the refrigeration cars for their ability to save lives.

With the war dragging on and the tide beginning to turn against Germany, the Kühlwagen was confronted with an increasing number of dangers. Allied forces, now better equipped and more determined, launched relentless attacks on rail supply lines. The refrigeration cars, once symbols of hope and resilience, now became prime targets. Captain Müller, now a seasoned veteran, saw the writing on the wall. Yet he remained committed to his duty, ensuring that every shipment went out.

The war ended in May 1945, and the Kühlwagen, like much of the German war machine was scrapped. They scrapped or repurposed many of them, causing their once-proud legacy to fade into the annals of history. Yet the impact of the refrigeration rail cars remained, a testament to German ingenuity and determination.

For Müller, Weiss, Fischer, and countless other Nazis, the Kühlwagen's were more than just machines. They saw the boxcar as a symbol of what could be accomplished through innovation. In a world torn apart by war, they had provided a good measure of hope and humanity. For one American serviceman the might provide a means of protection and escape.

# CHAPTER 7

## Trapped!
### *The Big Freeze*

*"Once you believe things are permanent,
you're trapped in a world without doors!"*
Genesis Orridge

For as long as he could remember, Private Jimmy Donovan had found himself falling asleep to the soothing sound of steel wheels rubbing against iron tracks. Before he was a member of the United States Army, he'd traveled throughout the vast American continent on a multitude of trains, and the repetitive sound had been his constant companion throughout these long journeys. This train ride, in the early spring of 1943 after the harshest winter in 100 years, may be his final one.

One of his orders was to make sure that the cargo did not arrive at its destination. It was a straightforward error that started all the trouble. Donovan found the boxcar open. In order to avoid being discovered, he climbed inside and then shut the door behind him. The interior of the boxcar was completely black. The faint beam of Jimmy's flashlight illuminated the rows of shelves that were still stocked with a few semi-frozen items as he searched the boxcar. He let out a breath, and the icy air caused him to leave a mist. His task had to be done swiftly. In the process of searching through the cartons, his fingers became numb. As he looked for anything of importance, each second seemed like a lifetime to him. But there was nothing—just food supplies for the long winter.

As the train suddenly lurched forward Jimmy lost his balance. He held onto a shelf, steadying himself as the train started move. The door slammed shut behind him with a resolute and uncompromising clang as soon as he successfully entered, with the lock clicking in a very menacing manner. Panic set in. Although he needed to get out, the door was now completely shut and locked from the outside. There was a remnant of his obsessive demand for completeness that led him to

walk into the refrigerated car to assess the cargo in the first place. It was icy, gloomy, and packed with empty food barrels and containers.

As Jimmy tried to get out, the handle refused to budge. In a low voice, he asked himself sarcastically, "OK what are we going to do now, Sarge?" His thoughts were racing, but the most important thing at the moment was to maintain his composure and locate a way out. Donovan felt a sense of panic as he realized he was trapped. The fear in his chest grew like a small flame that quickly grows into an inferno. Unaware of his predicament, the train continued to rumble along. The din of the railway engine, the howling wind, and the relentless scrape of metal on metal made it impossible for any of his adversaries to hear him even if they were just outside the boxcar.

"Surely I'm going to freeze to death and die in this damn boxcar," said the trapped Sergeant.

Spotting a coal fragment on the floor, he proceeded to write a final message on the Boxcar wall.

*"Got separated from unit, gonna freeze to death. Please tell family I love them! J"*

Jimmy's attempt to push or pry the door open was unsuccessful and the massive steel and tight lock remained stedfast. In a low voice, he asked himself, "So what ya gonna do now, Sarge?" While taking deep breaths his thoughts were racing, but the most important thing at the moment was to maintain his composure and locate a way out.

There was a dim light coming in through the gaps in the metal and wood slats of the boxcar and Jimmy's eyes adjusted. Like the bars of a primitive cage, the rough-hewn boards that were darkened with age and grime encircled him like a confinement system. He searched for any

indications of weakness by tracing the surface of the worn surface with his fingers. There was a musty odor that permeated the air inside, which was accompanied by the scent of rusting metal and old wood clung to his skin and clothes.

Hours passed. Although it was cold inside the car, the temperature was not below freezing. Jimmy was unaware of the fact that the refrigeration system had been malfunctioning for several months, which had resulted in the interior being cold but still livable. Yet, as the hours drew on, James felt the profound frost penetrated into his bones. His breath came in ragged, waves, each exhale a visible evidence to rising terror in his mind that cold might kill him.

In the stifling darkness of the freezer boxcar, Donovan's thoughts twisted into a hazardous cycle. During the harsh winters, he recalled hearing stories from his fellow soldiers about men who had died from freezing to death. Their bodies were found to be rigid and pale, and their faces were contorted in agony. At this moment, he could identify them as spectral beings that were dancing on the periphery of his vision, teasing him with their mute misery. He started to experience a chilling sensation. Every tremor and shiver that he experienced in his body seemed to validate his worst fears. The fabric of his jacket felt flimsy and ineffective against the growing cold that he imagined, so he drew it tightly about him.

Remembering the harsh nights spent in the trenches, the frostbite that claimed fingers and toes, and the numbness that spread like a poison, his mind, which was now a fertile field for terror, brought up recollections of those times. James's heart hammered in his chest, each beat a drum heralding his destiny. He attempted to relax himself, reciting the training mantras that had seen him through conflict in the past: "Stay focused. Stay vigilant. You are stronger than your worries!" But the words felt hollow, their power sapped by the encroaching darkness and cold.

As he plunged deeper into his mind's maze, he could no longer discern between reality and delusion. He felt the phantom touch of frost creeping up his limbs, the icy grip tightening around his chest. His thoughts turned to his comrades who had fallen in battle, their faces etched with the same icy fear he now mirrored.

Time lost meaning. It was a cruel reminder of James's isolation that his watch had stopped working, and its hands had frozen in place where they had been. His thoughts wandered to his family back in the house, the anxious expressions on his mother's face, and the stern but loving advice that his father gave him. As he sat alone in the dark, he pictured them receiving the news of his passing, their sorrow being a palpable force that threatened to crush him even now.

He started having hallucinations. The darkness of the rail car began to take on various forms, and shadows began to transform into silhouettes of people from his past. An old friend of his, Charlie, who'd passed away in North Africa, appeared before him. His face was pale and blue, and his lips whispered words that James could not comprehend. He saw his commanding officer, stern and unyielding, shaking his head in disappointment.

The cold in his mind became real. His body, though not truly freezing, reacted to the imagined chill. He curled into a fetal posture, attempting to save what little warmth he imagined he had left. His breathing grew shallow, each gasp a desperate attempt to draw air into lungs that felt like they were encased in ice.

Jimmy's mind kept replaying the horrors he had witnessed. The screams of dying soldiers, the silent tears of friends lost too soon, and the endless, bone-chilling nights in the trenches all melded into one continuous nightmare. He was trapped in a mental loop, his fear feeding on itself... growing stronger with each passing hour.

As the train thundered on through Italy and towards Germany, James's body began to shut down. His mind, convinced of the lethal cold, triggered a physiological response. He experienced a relaxation of his blood vessels, a slowing of his heart rate, and a decrease in his body temperature. Under the influence of a p s y c h o l o g i c a l hypothermia, he was experiencing a lethal illusion that he had concocted by his own thoughts. His bones began to feel the chill, and he  huddled in a corner, wrapping his arms around himself to protect himself from the cold. He had to stay calm, had to keep his mind focused. But the icy grip of fear tightened around him. The psychological toll of his entrapment was severe. Donovan knew that the mind could play tricks.

To escape from the locked boxcar Donovan began with a systematic approach. He examined the door mechanism, sometimes, doors can be jammed but not locked. He looked for any levers, latches, or handles that might release the door. When that didn't work, he began looking for Tools. He search the boxcar for any tools or objects that could help you open the door, such as crowbars, metal rods, or anything sturdy that can pry the door open or loosen a floor board. He began searching for weak points inspecting the structure of the boxcar for any areas that might be easier to break through, such as panels, vents, or windows. Most of all he reminded himself to stay calm and keep a clear head. Panicking might make it tougher to think properly and find a solution.

He had been on the move for what felt like hours, the relentless motion of the train becoming a physical ache in his bones. Donovan's mind raced as he plotted his escape. The door was the most obvious exit, but also the most challenging. Heavy and bolted from the outside, it would not yield. He needed another way.

The first step was to find a tool—anything that could help him pry open the door or create an opening elsewhere. He scanned the boxcar, his eyes finally settling on a rusted metal rod lying in a corner. It looked like it'd been part of some forgotten machinery left to decay in the car. Jimmy picked it up, feeling its weight, testing its strength. It would have to do.

He moved closer to the entrance with a resolute expression. The metal rod slipped into the narrow gap between the door and its frame, and he began to move it back and forth. The metal groaned in protest, the sound mingling with the clatter of the train. He poured all his strength into it, his muscles straining, his breath coming in ragged gasps. But the door was stubborn, refusing to budge. Frustration gnawed at him. He couldn't give up.

Abandoning the door for the moment, Donovan turned his attention to the walls. He ran his hands over the boards, feeling for any signs of looseness. One plank near the back of the car wobbled slightly under his touch. His heart quickened. He wedged the metal rod into the space beside the plank and pried it slowly. The wood resisted. After a short while Donovan's hands were raw and bleeding. He'd need to find another option. There had to be a way.

He gazed upward to the ceiling. The boxcar's roof was reinforced with metal beams, but there were also gaps between them. Maybe, just maybe, he could climb up and find a way out through the top. It was a long shot, but he had no other options. He started by stacking crates and boxes he found scattered around the car, creating a makeshift ladder. Each box was a precarious step, wobbling under his weight. He steadied himself, focusing on his balance. The ceiling seemed a distant, impossible goal, but it had a small hatch and he was determined to reach it. Finally, he grasped one of the metal beams, his fingers curling around the cold steel. He had almost pulled himself up,

muscles straining, and was hanging from the beam. The train sped along the tracks, the countryside a blur he clung to the ceiling but when the train hit its next bump he lost his grip falling to the floor of the railway car and breaking his leg.

More hours passed, and as the pain set in the temperature seemed to drop even further. Jimmy's thoughts moved inward, his mind playing games on him. He envisioned the ice crawling up his limbs, the cold taking the life out of him. His breaths came in frantic gasps, each one more terrible than the last.

His education had prepared him for a variety of situations, but not for this one. Everything was too much, including the cold and the isolation. He thought of his family back home, of the warmth of his mother's kitchen, the laughter of his siblings. He clung to these memories, trying to stave off the chill. But the cold was relentless. Jimmy's body shook uncontrollably, his teeth chattering. He could feel his heartbeat slowing, the frostbite spreading. He closed his eyes, imagining he was back home, safe and warm. As hours turned into a day, the Kühlwagen remained a prison taking Donovan deeper into enemy territory. The rhythmic clattering of the wheels on the tracks was a cruel reminder of his predicament.

Jimmy tried to stand, but his legs wouldn't support him. His intellect had convinced his body of its fate. Eyesight blurred as he collapsed on the floor of the oil vehicle. He lay there, his body shaking, his breath short. All he could feel was the cold, the harsh, unrelenting cold. Jimmy's thoughts began to wander to his new wife as the night drew closer, and then they moved on to his fellow soldiers and the mission that he'd failed to complete. He was furious that the cold had defeated him, although he had come so close. As the train journeyed through Italy, now occupied by the Nazis, Donovan's thoughts turned to survival. He searched the car for anything that could help him escape, but the interior offered no solutions.

In his last hours, James found a strange clarity. He saw his life in flashes: his childhood home, the rolling fields of his family's farm, the warm embrace of his mother, the stern but loving guidance of his father. He remembered his first day in the Army, the pride he felt wearing the uniform, and the camaraderie he felt with his fellow soldiers. It was nice to belong.

He laughed to himself when he remembered playing Army as a kid back in Ohio. Young Jimmy Donovan, all of 12 years old, crouched, clutching a stick that served as his rifle. He and his friends were deep in the woods behind his house, their playground transformed into a battleground where imagination reigned supreme. Jimmy's heart raced with excitement as he peered through the underbrush, envisioning himself as a brave soldier on a daring mission. The world around him faded away, leaving only the thrill of adventure and the camaraderie of his friends, their laughter and shouts echoing through the trees.

In his mind, Jimmy was always the hero, leading his squad through perilous terrain, his stick-turned-rifle held high as they charged the imaginary enemy. The woods were alive with the sounds of battle: the crack of twigs underfoot, the rustle of leaves in the wind, and the triumphant cries of his comrades. Each movement was deliberate, every step calculated, as they crept through their makeshift battlefield, their youthful energy transforming the familiar landscape into a place of endless possibilities. Jimmy's imagination painted the world in vivid colors, his heart swelling with the thrill of being part of something grand and important. Something bigger than himself.

He thought of Mary, the girl he married before shipping out for the war. Her grin, her laughter, the way her eyes lighted up when she saw him. He could almost hear her voice, a comforting song in the darkness. "Come back to me, James," she would plead. But now somehow he knew that the fates would not all it and he wouldn't be returning. As he lost consciousness again he flashed back to the first time he kissed her... The late afternoon Ohio sun dipped below the horizon, painting the sky in hues of pink and gold as Jimmy Donovan and Mary O'Connor strolled along the quiet path by the river. The world around them seemed to slow down, the gentle rustling of leaves and the soft murmur of the water fading into the background. Jimmy's heart raced as he glanced at Mary, her auburn hair catching the last rays of sunlight, and he felt a familiar warmth spreading through him. They paused at the edge of the riverbank, the air heavy with unspoken words.

Mary turned to Jimmy, her eyes sparkling with a mixture of mischief and something deeper. "You know, Jimmy," she said softly, "I've always wondered why you haven't kissed me yet." Her words hung in the air, a gentle challenge wrapped in a smile that sent his heart into overdrive. He swallowed, suddenly aware of the distance between them, a mere whisper of space that felt both insurmountable and inviting. Gathering his courage, Jimmy reached for her hand and he felt a jolt of electricity shoot up his arm.

As the first stars began to twinkle in the evening sky, Jimmy leaned in, his breath mingling with Mary's, and captured her lips in a tender, tentative kiss. It was as if the world around them faded away, leaving only the two of them in a universe of their own making. Her lips were soft and warm against his, and in that fleeting moment, Jimmy felt as though he had discovered something profound and beautiful. When they finally parted, their eyes met, a silent promise passing between them, sealing a memory that would linger long

after the stars had vanished. He woke the next morning not sure where he was.

For the third day in a row as the train continued on, Donovan was again left alone with his thoughts, and he experienced the oppressive weight of being isolated. He could not shake the feeling that he was about to die from the cold. As he allowed his thoughts to wander, he experienced a profound sense of peace. Suddenly, the fear and panic that had been consuming him for several hours dissipated, and in its place came a serene acceptance. It was then that his thoughts turned to the men he had served alongside, those who had sacrificed their lives for their honor and country.

When confronted with death, he experienced a sense of kinship with them, a shared bond. Despite the temperature being above freezing, Donovan's mind began deceiving him. He imagined frost forming on the walls, felt his limbs growing numb. The psychological impact of his entrapment was as real as any physical threat. His sense advised him to be sensible, but the darkness was unrelenting.

As Jimmy lay on the cold, hard floor of the railway boxcar, his breath coming in shallow, labored gasps, his mind drifted through a haze of memories and regrets. The rhythmic clatter of the train wheels seemed to echo the beat of his fading heart, a steady, unrelenting reminder of the life slipping away from him. In those final moments, his thoughts turned to Mary, her image vivid and clear amid the fog of pain. He recalled the way her laughter had filled the room, her eyes sparkling with life and love, and how she had held him so tightly before he left. Her face was his anchor, a warm beacon in the encroaching darkness, and he clung to the memory of their time together with a desperate hope that it might somehow transcend the distance between them.

Images from his past flickered through his mind like a montage, moments of joy and sorrow, victories and losses. He remembered his childhood games of playing soldier, the innocence of those days now a cruel irony. His friends, many lost to the war, appeared in brief, poignant flashes, their laughter echoing in the recesses of his memory. He wondered what might have been if the world had not been torn apart by conflict, if he and his comrades could have lived out their lives in peace. Yet, amid the reflections, there was a profound sense of acceptance. Jimmy realized that he had done his duty, fought bravely alongside brothers and that his sacrifice was part of something larger.

As the shadows deepened, Jimmy felt a strange calm settle over him, a release from the pain and fear that had gripped him. He focused on Mary once more, silently sending his love across the miles that separated them. He hoped she would somehow feel his presence, know that she had been his greatest joy and that their love was the light that had guided him through the darkest days. With a final, faltering breath, he let go, surrendering to the stillness that promised peace, holding on to the belief that, somewhere beyond this world, they would meet again.

James's final thoughts were of gratitude. For the life he had lived, for the love he had known, and for the courage he had found within himself, even in the face of unimaginable fear. He took one last breath, his body relaxing into the icy embrace of the freezer car. He closed his eyes. The train rumbled into the night, the noise fading into the distance. Jimmy lay still, the cold covering him like a blanket in the unforgiving night. His last breath was just a whisper. And then... silence. The Kühlwagen, once a marvel of German engineering, had now become a tomb.

# CHAPTER 8

## The Letter
### *One Last Goodbye*

*"Letters are among the most significant memorial
a person can leave behind."*
World War 2 Chaplin

On so many different levels, the war was a
catastrophe, but it was especially devastating for
young lovers. According to Jimmy Donovan and
Mary Cooper, who found themselves brought
together by the currents of fate, the place where the
sun stays in the azure skies of summer longer than
it does anyplace else on the earth is in the middle
of Ohio farm country. They were two souls making
their way through the delicate transition from
childhood to adulthood, and their lives came
together in the picturesque Town of Albion.

Jimmy, his hair kissed by the sun and his blue eyes
radiating sincerity, personified being the boy-next-
door. Everyone knew him for his sense of humor
and the ever-present touch of mischief that danced
in his smile. He grew up on a humble corn and
cow farm on the outskirts of town and gained
notoriety for his successes on the football field.
Lady Mary was the epitome of elegance and allure.
Her laughter reverberated through the fields like
the promise of tomorrow, and her hazel eyes

conveyed a depth that suggested she had dreams she hadn't achieved yet.

It was at the local five and dime soda fountain, where Jimmy was working part time to save money for college, that they first met. The melody of laughter and banter that Mary brought with her as she entered the room attracted Jimmy. A group of friends joined her. Although he couldn't help but steal looks at her, he admired the seamless way in which she combined warmth and confidence.

After what seemed like an eternity, their eyes finally met with intent. It was a scorching afternoon in July. Jimmy, using a rag that had seen better days to clean the counter, looked up to discover Mary standing by herself close to the jukebox. With a worried smile on his face, he approached her, feeling emboldened by a burst of courage he didn't know he possessed.

As he greeted her he said, "Hey there," but his tone of voice betrayed his attempt to be casual.

Mary looked around, and her smile became wider as she recognized the sincere young man who had frequently captured her attention while she was out and about in town. She replied, "Hello," in a voice that was gentle and musical, like a summer breeze.

They exchanged niceties that quickly gave way to casual chat. Jimmy learnt Mary was an aspiring artist, her sketches capturing aspects of ordinary life with a touch of whimsy. Mary was the one who found Jimmy's enthusiasm for literature. His love for Hemingway and Faulkner became the spark that ignited passionate conversations between them that sometimes lasted for several hours.

Their connection grew stronger amid the backdrop of starry skies and sun-dappled afternoons as the days turned into weeks and the weeks expanded into months. And as Europe started done the path of war the sound of their laughter blended with the cacophony of crickets and cicadas as they strolled across fields of wildflowers in Ohio. With each passing day, they seemed to grow closer as they shared moments together. These times created a strong understanding and affection between them.

He invited her to the dance that Saturday night. The night was alive with the infectious rhythm of big band music, the lively notes of a trumpet soaring above the syncopated beat of drums and bass. Jimmy Donovan held Mary O'Connor in his arms, feeling the warmth of her presence as they glided across the dance floor. The dim glow of the club's lights cast a golden hue over the scene, making everything seem magical and dreamlike. For a few precious moments, the world outside faded away, the war just a distant echo, overshadowed by their music and laughter.

Mary's laugh was a melody all its own, bright and carefree, as she spun under Jimmy's guiding hand.

Her dress twirled with her, a vibrant splash of color in the sea of dancers. Jimmy couldn't help but smile, his heart lightened by her presence and the ease with which they moved together. The music seemed to lift them off their feet, and each step felt like a celebration of life and love, a defiant dance against the uncertainty of the times. In that moment, everything felt possible, as if the world outside didn't exist.

As the song drew to a close, Jimmy pulled Mary closer, their eyes meeting in a silent acknowledgment of the fleeting nature of their happiness. The war might separate them, but tonight was theirs, a brief respite from the chaos. The band struck up another tune, and they joined the other couples once more, losing themselves in the music. Dancing with Mary, Jimmy felt a sense of hope for the future, a reminder that even in the darkest times, moments of joy could be found and should be cherished

Despite the fact that their growing romance was filled with sweetness, there were hints of doubt and trouble hiding on the horizon. Because Jimmy had aspirations that took him to faraway lands where he could fulfill his duty and preserve his honor, he had dreams that went beyond the boundaries of Ohio. And Mary, whose heart was brimming with artistic aspirations, pondered whether love could withstand the storms of uncertainty and war in Europe of the Pacific looming on the path before the both of them.

However, for the time being, Jimmy and Mary discovered that the straightforward passion of their love brought them the fulfillment they were looking for. They knew that whatever the future held, they would face it together, united by a love that grew like the fields of Ohio under the June sun. As they stood hand in hand beneath the enormous oak tree that had watched their journey, they were aware of the fact that America would not sit out the war forever. It couldn't stand by, not after the attack of December 7th by Japan.

To him, it seemed like a lifetime ago when he was thinking about that simple time with Mary when love was new. After a few years passed, Jimmy, now trapped inside a rail car belonging to the Nazis, with his leg fractured and his body almost frozen, tried to stay positive. But as he lost consciousness he flashed back to the last time he spoke to his love, Mary, in a phone call from the base right before shipping out.

Jimmy's barracks were quiet, the hum of nervous energy almost palpable. Soldiers milled about, packing their gear, writing last letters home, or staring into space, lost in their own thoughts. Jimmy Donovan, after being in line for an hour, stood at the payphone, its black receiver heavy in his hand. He took a deep breath, then dialed the familiar number in Ohio.

"Hello?" Mary's voice was soft, a gentle reminder of everything he was leaving behind.

"Hey, Lover girl it's me," Jimmy said, trying to keep his voice positive and casual.

"Jimmy!" Her voice brightened, but he could hear the worry beneath the surface. "I was hoping maybe you'd call."

"Yeah, well, you know I couldn't leave without talking to you," he said, leaning against the wall. "We're shipping out soon."

"I know, I got your letter." Mary replied, her voice tinged with sadness. "I've been thinking about you every single day. How are you holding up?"

Jimmy glanced around the barracks, the sight of his comrades offering little comfort. "As good as can be, I guess. Everyone's on edge, but we're ready. Or as ready as we'll ever be. We're gonna give them Nazis the dickens!"

There was a pause, the silence filled with the weight of unspoken fears. "I wish you didn't have to go," Mary said finally, her voice trembling slightly. "I wish you could stay here with me."

"Me too, Mary, me too" Jimmy said, his heart aching at the thought. "But this is something I must do. You know that, right?"

"I do," she sighed. "I just... I'm scared, Jimmy. What if something happens to you?"

He closed his eyes, wishing he could be there to hold her, to reassure her. "Let's leave it in God's hands and I'll do everything I can to come back to you my love. I promise."

"Just be safe, okay? And write to me whenever you can. I'll be waiting for your letters and I will write you every week," she said.

"I will," Jimmy said, the words feeling inadequate. "And you take care of yourself, too. Keep busy, stay with friends. No time worrying, OK?"

"I'll try," she said, her voice a little stronger. "Just come back to me, Jimmy. That's all I want."

"I will," he repeated, wishing he could believe it as completely as he wanted her to. "I love you, Mary. Please always remember that!"

"I love you too, Jimmy. Sooooo much," she said.

There was another pause, the moment stretching out as if neither wanted to let go. Finally, Jimmy spoke. "I've got to go. I'm a popular guy," he joked. "Take care, Mary. No worries. I'll see you soon."

"Goodbye, Jimmy. Please come back safely to me young man. I love you, you know!" she said.

"I will. I love you too baby girl, bye, bye."

He slowly hung up the phone, the click of the receiver echoing in his ears. For a moment, he stood there, letting the weight of the call settle over

him. Then he turned, squaring his shoulders, and walked back to his bunk. The road ahead was uncertain, and Mary's voice lingered in his mind, a beacon of hope and a motivator to stay safe. Sometimes at times like these Donovan wished he had joined the supply corps!

As he regained consciousness the young Sergeant realized that things were not taking a positive turn. He decided a last letter to the woman who had been the love of his life was presently his best option. As the train wound its way through the Italian night with his last ounce of strength, Sgt. Jimmy Donovan, took out his pencil, which was now really just a stub, and a small US Army issued note pad to write one last farewell to his new wife.

*Italy, Winter 1944*
*My Love,*

*By accident, I've locked myself in. It's one of those brand-new refrigerator cars associated with the Nazi party. In the morning, I think I am gonna be dead from the cold. As horrible as this all is it sure is better than being surrounded by the sounds of artillery and the cries of my brothers, Now my thoughts turn to you, as I sit here with a bum leg in a cold railroad boxcar. I'm locked in here with no way out. Every day I miss you more during this damn war. If you got this it's a sign I'm no longer here. But even if I'm not physically present with you, I want you to know that my soul will always be by your and Jack's side. Dearest Mary, you've been my rock and the reason I've been able to persevere. Your letters, with their careful handwriting (haha) and words of encouragement, have really been my savior. Sorry I wasn't able to*

*make that happen for us. I have no regrets and I'm
proud to be here. Our little Jack is growing up, and
I sure wish I could be there to watch him grow.
Please tell him stories about me, about how much
his Daddy loved him. Take care of him, like you've
always taken care of me. My only regret, my love,
is not being able to spend the rest of my life with
you. Please know that I fought for our freedoms
and a better future not only for us but also our son.
Our love transcends time and distance, I'll be
there to help you through the hard times. I'll see
you again in heaven!
All My Love Always,
Jimmy*

He laid down his pencil, folded the note, placing it
in the front pocket of his fatigues over his heart.
He did this hoping they would discover it on his
body and present it to her personally.

The bravery, love, and acceptance of fate that
Donovan displayed was characterized by the fact
he found solace in the recollections of better times.
Without the slightest basis in logic, he thought his
sacrifice would not be in vain. His letter serves as
a powerful reminder of the human cost of war and
the eternal power of love, even in the face of death.
As he wrote it he firmly believed that he'd be dead
by morning and unfortunately his mind was busy
figuring out how to make that happen!

*Troops from the 101st Airborne arrive to secure the liberated rail station where both Giovanni had worked for years and where the body of Sgt. Jimmy Donovan was discovered in a rail car.*

# CHAPTER 9

## The Next Day
### *Frozen in Ultimate Sacrifice*

*"Cold is merciless. It shows you
where you are. What you are."*
Wim Hof

The process of hypothermia, sometimes known as freezing to death, is typically painless; in fact, several people have characterized it as an experience similar to falling asleep. It results from multiple steps.

In the beginning, you experience a sensation of extreme coldness as your body temperature falls below the normal range. Your body attempts to generate heat through involuntary muscular contractions, sometimes known as shivering, in order to maintain temperature. It's possible that you will experience a loss of sensation in your extremities (hands, feet) as your body temperature continues to plummet. Because of the cold, your brain function may become compromised, which can lead to feelings of confusion and disorientation. Donovan was front row to it.

When your body's trying to preserve energy, your heart rate and respiratory rate both decrease down. This is a stage at which intervention is required in order to stop the condition from deteriorating any further. As your essential organs, particularly the heart, struggle to operate in the extreme cold, you may eventually lose consciousness. This is because of the extreme cold exposure. In the absence of immediate medical action to warm the body and restore normal function, death can occur because of cardiac arrest or organ failure not being performed. It's a progressive process in which the systems of the body shut down because of the inability to maintain a core temperature that is compatible with life.

Four days later the train arrived at the very same station Donovan had met Giovanni at about a week before. Small world. The Allies had liberated it just days before. The Germans had escaped and left everything behind. When they opened all the boxcars, they discovered Jimmy's body. The medics saw that there was no evidence of frostbite and that there were no outward manifestations of hypothermia. It appeared as though he had simply given up, his mind giving in to the cold that appeared to be present but was not actually present. The medical examiner would be presented with a conundrum: a guy who appeared to have succumbed to hypothermia despite being in a boxcar that never reached freezing temperatures.

James Donovan had been a prisoner of his worst imaginings and deepest anxieties throughout his whole life. He hade always had an overactive imagination. But the truth was more insidious than that: his own mind had slain him. His death was a striking reminder of the power of the human mind, its ability to mold reality, and the fine line between life and death. In the end, it was not the Nazis or the cold that had ended his life, but the icy grip of his own thoughts.

The final thoughts that James had were ones of gratitude. Regarding the life that he had lived, the love that he had experienced, and the bravery that he had discovered in himself, even in the face of fear that was beyond his comprehension. As he took his final breath, his body relaxed into the icy embrace of the freezer car to complete the process.

The process of hypothermia, which is also referred to as freezing to death, is typically painless. In fact, several individuals have described it as a sensation that's comparable to how one might feel while they are falling asleep. A feeling of acute coldness, which occurs when your body temperature goes below the usual range characterizes the initial phase of the condition. Your body makes attempts to generate heat by involuntary muscle contractions, which are frequently referred to as shivering in order to maintain temperature. As your body temperature continues to drop, it's conceivable that you'll start to feel a loss of sensation in your extremities (hands, feet).

It's possible that the cold will cause your brain function to become impaired, which may cause feelings of confusion and disorientation. To conserve energy, your heart rate and respiratory rate both slow down. This is because your body is trying to conserve energy. Intervention is essential at this critical stage in order to prevent the situation from deteriorating any further. This stage is crucial. Exposure to extremely low temperatures may cause your vital organs, particularly your heart, to struggle with functioning, potentially leading to a loss of consciousness. In the absence of prompt medical intervention to warm the body and restore normal function, it's possible for a person to pass away because of cardiac arrest or organ failure. Because of the inability to keep a core body temperature that's suitable for life, a progressive process in which the systems of the body begin to shut down. This is from an inability to maintain a core body temperature.

**On the fourth day,** the train came to a halt at a German supply depot. Unbeknownst to Donovan an Allied air raid had targeted the rail yard 2 days before. Within the midst of the mayhem, a group of Italian resistance fighters who were operating in the region took advantage of the opportunity to launch an attack. Claire Gavichi, the woman who coordinated the resistance fighters, brought to their attention that the Kühlwagen was transporting Nazi supplies. As they moved through the yard, they came upon the refrigerator car, broke the lock

*Donovan's train came in*

and opened the door. There Donovan lay. The Kühlwagen, once a symbol of German logistical might, had become a place of torment and death for the young soldier.

When they found him, his body was cold but not frozen. The medical examiner would note the paradox: a man who appeared to have died from hypothermia in a car that never dropped below freezing. James Donovan had been a prisoner of his darkest imaginings and deepest fears, and his own mind had killed him. The truth was more insidious than most people realize.

The Germans had retreated abandoning everything. The Allies had freed the train's final destination and by morning it pulled into a station previously held by the Nazis. Car by car, the Allied troops carefully inspected the train boxcars. As they searched the train they opened the last boxcar, coming across the body of Sgt. James 'Jimmy' Donovan of Ohio. It appeared he had frozen to death, however upon further inspection of the train car's refrigeration unit, it was discovered to be faulty, and "due to the local weather conditions, the temperature inside the car never fell below 40°!" the Medic explained. It was the strangest death most in Army medicine had ever seen.

At the military morgue the medical personnel observed that there was no real evidence of frostbite, and no obvious signs of hypothermia. At lease none visible to the naked eye. It appeared he had just given up. His mind seemed to have given in to the cold that seemed to be present but was not actually present. The circumstances surrounding his death were bought to the attention of the medical examiner. Here was a man who appeared to have died from hypothermia while riding in a boxcar that never fell below freezing. How was that possible?

Throughout his life, James Donovan had sometimes been a captive of his worst fears and most agonizing thoughts. The reality was even more nefarious than that: his own thoughts had killed him. Donovan's passing served as a striking reminder of the power the human mind possesses, its capacity to shape reality, and the thin line that separates life and death. In the end, it wasn't the freezing cold, but the icy grip of his own thoughts that first crippled him and then killed him.

As he lay there on the floor of that Italian Boxcar with its broken refrigeration unit, Jimmy was filled with feelings of gratitude. As he reflected on the life he had lived, the love that he had experienced, and the bravery that he had discovered within himself, he found peace even in the face of fear. It was beyond his comprehension that he was to die like this. His body finally sank into the embrace of the boxcar as he exhaled his last breath.

After the war and his death Donovan was honored as a decorated hero. He received the Bronze Star for his bravery in combat. He carried with him the values and lessons learned during his service and years before on a small Ohio farm. The funeral of Sgt. James Donovan, an Ohio native was held with honors at Arlington National Cemetery in Washington, District of Columbia. To serve as a constant reminder of the battles fought not only with firearms and bullets but also with the mind and spirit, they engraved his name into the roll of the fallen. Sadly his body was lost in transit from the war zone and he was not able to be fully buried. As time went on, Jack, Donovan's son, became a high school teacher and used his Dad's

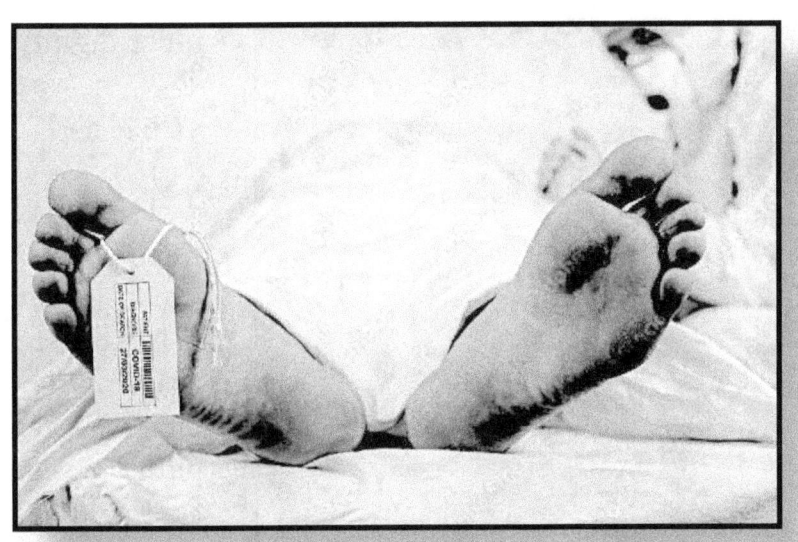

experiences to inspire and educate future generations about America's sacrifices in WWII.

The Tomb of the Unknown Soldier at Arlington National Cemetery stands as a solemn tribute to those who have given their lives in service without recognition. Situated on a hillside overlooking the capital, the marble monument is striking in its simplicity and grandeur. The tomb is guarded around the clock by sentinels from the US Army's 3rd Infantry Regiment, known as "The Old Guard." They patrol the site 24/7 with a precision that reflects our nation's reverence for the fallen. The site evokes a sense of timeless honor and respect, drawing visitors who come to pay their respects and reflect on the sacrifices made.

Each guard change at the tomb is a poignant ceremony, performed with meticulous care and

quiet dignity. The sentinel's slow, deliberate steps echo in the hushed silence as they walk their 21-step path, pause for 21 seconds, then turn and repeat, symbolizing the highest military honor. This ritual is a powerful reminder of the commitment to remember those who served anonymously, without the recognition given to others. The sentinels' dedication through all weather and seasons embodies the nation's gratitude, a living testament to never to forgetting the sacrifices made by these unknown soldiers.

The inscription on the tomb reads, *"Here rests in honored glory an American soldier known but to God."* These words encapsulate the profound mystery and sacrifice represented by the tomb. The presence of visitors,

whether they're veterans, families, or tourists from around the world, speaks to the universal resonance of this monument. In this sacred space, the division between the past and present blurs, allowing a shared moment of reflection on the price of war and the lives it claims. The tomb stands not only as a memorial to the unknown but also as a symbol of the bond between a nation and its soldiers and veterans.

With a missing body his family was only able to have a memorial ceremony for Sgt. James Donovan. Whispers of speculation sometimes floated through the small town where he'd once lived, a place now forever marked by his absence. To those who remembered him—his quick smile, his unwavering sense of duty—the mystery surrounding the Tomb of the Unknown Soldier began to hold a particular poignancy.

As stories of anonymous heroes emerged, some locals couldn't help but wonder if Jimmy, whose body vanished after being found dead in the Nazi boxcar, might indeed be the one laid to rest in that hallowed monument. It was a notion both comforting and sort of haunting, imagining that their lost son, husband, or friend could be enshrined in eternal honor. His sacrifice symbolizes the many untold stories of valor from World War Two.

Though no confirmation could ever truly assuage their lingering grief, the possibility that Jimmy was the 'Unknown Solider' in Arlington offered some measure of solace, binding their collective memory. It'd be fitting to have Jimmy included in a national monument of remembrance like that. These soldiers were killed not only with firearms and bullets, but also with the human mind.

In the annals of history, Donovan's story is a symbol of the unseen wounds that war inflicts on soldiers and the silent struggles that soldiers face. And in the night's stillness those who remember the price that was paid for our freedoms still whisper his story.

# CHAPTER 10

## Mind Over Matter
### *The Real Killer*

*"Fortune favors the prepared mind."*
Dr. Louis Pasteur

The human mind is a powerful force, capable of shaping reality in profound ways. It can make a man believe he is freezing to death in a car that is barely cold. The Kühlwagen, though designed to preserve life by keeping food fresh, had become a grave for James, a stark reminder of the mind's power to both protect and destroy.

James's death was a testament to the fragile line between reality and perception. His body, reacting to the fear and stress, shut down in response to an imagined threat. The mind, in a quest to make sense of the darkness, created a deadly illusion.

In high-stress combat situations, the concept of "mind over matter"

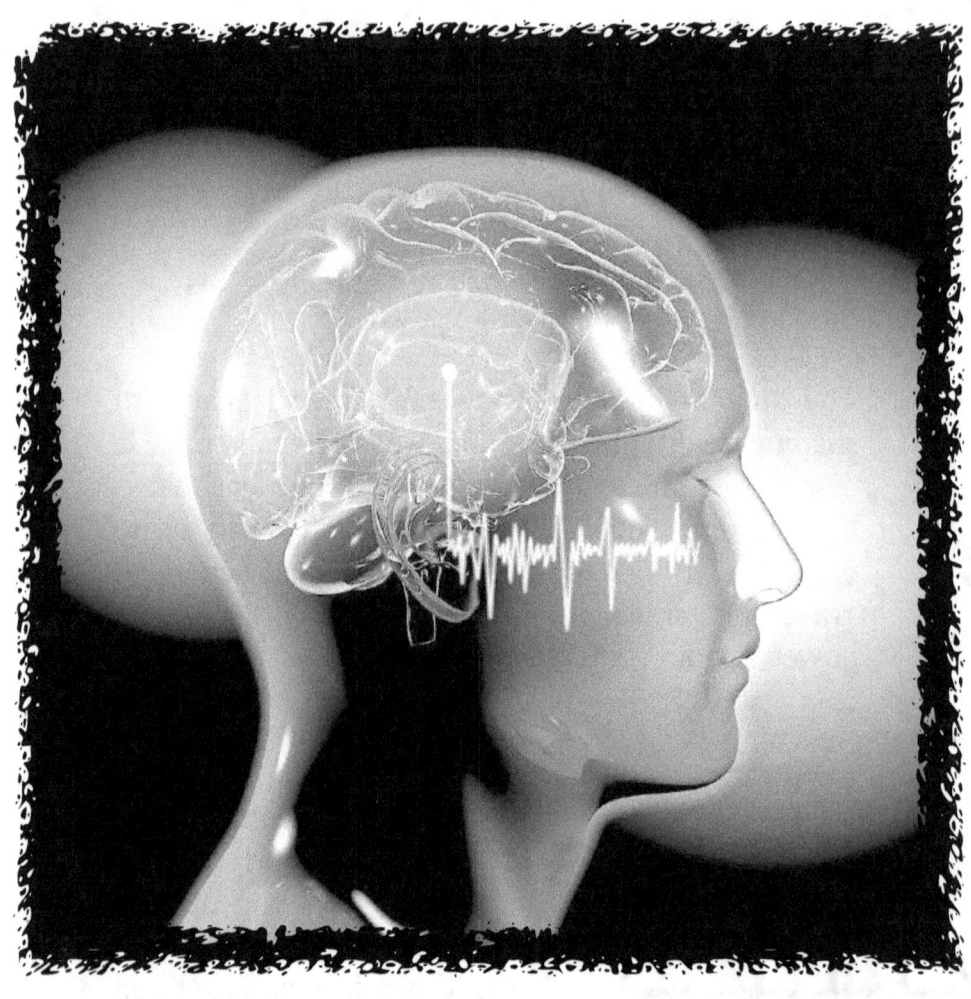

is often vividly illustrated. One notable example comes from the experiences of soldiers in World War II, such as those during the D-Day invasion on June 6, 1944. Amidst the chaos and danger of the Normandy landings, soldiers had to push through intense fear and physical exhaustion. The mental fortitude required to keep moving forward under heavy fire, despite the omnipresent threat of death, is a stark demonstration of mind over matter. Many soldiers reported that focusing on their training, their comrades, and their mission helped them to overcome paralyzing fear and continue to fight.

Another example is found in Vietnam, particularly among pilots who endured the harrowing experience of being shot down and captured as prisoners of war (POWs). The determination of men like Navy pilot John McCain, who survived years of torture and deprivation in the 'Hanoi Hilton,' showcases extraordinary mental strength. McCain's ability to maintain his will to survive, resist his captors, and emerge with his spirit intact highlights the real power of mental determination.

The power of the human mind is incredible and can significantly influence the body, but it cannot cause a person to literally freeze to death through thought alone. The idea of the mind inducing death by freezing hinges on the concept of psychosomatic effects, where psychological factors can lead to physical symptoms. However, there are limitations to what the mind can do to the body.

The concept of "mind over matter" encapsulates the remarkable influence our mental state can exert over our physical well-being. This idea suggests that through sheer willpower and positive thinking, one can overcome physical limitations and challenges. It's a principle seen in athletes who push through pain to achieve their goals, or in patients who recover more quickly when they maintain a positive outlook. The placebo effect is a prime example of this phenomenon, where a patient's belief in the efficacy of a treatment can lead to documented physiological improvements, even when treatment itself is inert.

Psychosomatic diseases further illustrate the profound connection between the mind and body. These conditions, where psychological factors play a significant role in the manifestation of physical symptoms, demonstrate how stress, anxiety, and other mental states can trigger or exacerbate physical ailments. Common examples include tension headaches, stomach ulcers, and irritable bowel syndrome. In these cases, the body's response to mental stressors can cause genuine physical discomfort and illness, highlighting the need for a holistic approach to health that considers both mental and physical well-being.

Understanding psychosomatic illness underscores the importance of addressing mental health to prevent and treat physical diseases. Therapies like cognitive-behavioral therapy (CBT) and mindfulness-based stress reduction (MBSR) have shown effectiveness in managing and alleviating symptoms of psychosomatic conditions. By teaching patients to manage their stress, reframe negative thoughts, and cultivate a calmer, more resilient mindset, these therapies help break the cycle of mental stress leading to physical symptoms. This holistic approach emphasizes that nurturing mental health is not just beneficial but essential for overall physical health.

In high-stress combat situations, the concept of "mind over matter" is often vividly illustrated. One notable example comes from the experiences of soldiers in World War II, such as those during the D-Day invasion on June 6, 1944. Amidst the chaos and danger of the Normandy landings, soldiers had to push through intense fear and physical exhaustion. The mental fortitude required to keep moving forward under heavy fire, despite the omnipresent threat of death, is a stark demonstration of mind over matter. Many soldiers reported that focusing on their training, their comrades, and their mission helped them to overcome paralyzing fear and continue to move forward on the beaches.

Another example is found in the Vietnam War, particularly among pilots who endured the harrowing experience of being shot down and captured as prisoners of war (POWs). The resilience of men like Navy pilot John McCain, who survived years of torture and deprivation in the "Hanoi Hilton," showcases extraordinary mental strength. McCain's ability to maintain his will to survive, resist his captors, and emerge with his spirit intact, highlights the profound power of mental determination over physical suffering.

More recently, the mental resilience of soldiers in modern conflicts like Iraq and Afghanistan, has been documented. Special Forces operators, like those in the US Navy SEALs, undergo rigorous mental conditioning alongside their physical training. Their ability to remain calm and focused under extreme stress, such as during the raid on Osama bin Laden's compound in 2011, exemplifies how psychological preparation and mental toughness enable troops to perform exceptionally in life-and-death situations. These examples collectively underscore the critical role that mental strength plays in overcoming the severe stress of combat.

There is a definite documented Mind-Body connection and Psychosomatic Disorders are but one example; chronic pain, gastrointestinal issues, and skin conditions that have no apparent physical cause are some examples. Stress and anxiety can exacerbate these symptoms, but they rarely result in life-threatening conditions. This is also the Nocebo Effect, a phenomenon where negative expectations about a treatment or condition can cause harmful effects. A sort of self-fulfilling prophecy. If a person believes they're taking poison, they might experience adverse symptoms even if the substance is inert.

The Nocebo Effect can significantly affect a person's well-being but is unlikely to cause death. There are Physiological Boundaries and the human

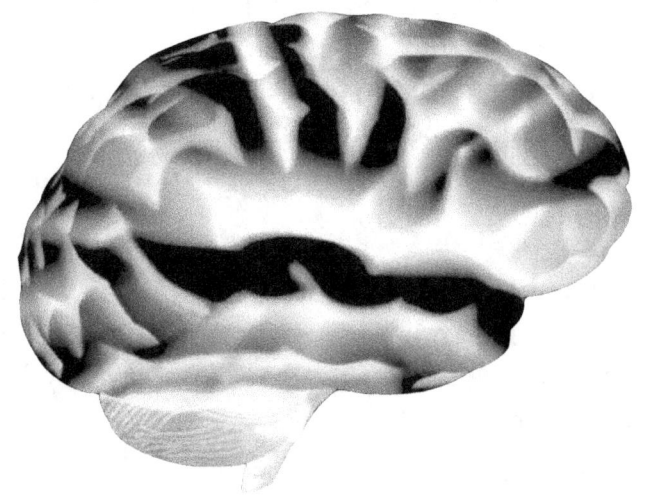

body has various homeostatic mechanisms that maintain essential functions such as body temperature regulation, heart rate, and breathing. While the mind can influence these to some extent (e.g., through meditation, stress responses), it cannot override them to the point of causing death by freezing in a mild environment. The body's natural defenses against cold, for example shivering is an automatic response that the mind can't fully suppress.

There are no documented cases where a person has died purely from the belief that they were freezing. Cases of hypothermia involve environmental factors that physically lower the body's temperature. Extreme psychological stress can lead to severe results like heart attacks, but this differs from the body being convinced it's freezing to death in normal temps.

The human mind has a remarkable capacity to influence the body, but it operates within certain physiological limits. While extreme psychological conditions can exacerbate physical symptoms, they can't induce death by hypothermia in normal environmental conditions.

Understanding the mind-body connection can lead to better management of psychosomatic conditions and overall health, but it also requires recognizing the boundaries of the mind's influence over the body. And this can be positive or negative.

The U.S. military Special Forces employ positive mental reinforcement as a cornerstone of their training regimen, understanding that mental resilience is as vital as physical prowess in preparing for combat. This approach focuses on reinforcing soldiers' belief in their capabilities and fostering a mindset that can withstand the pressures of battle. Through various psychological techniques, such as visualization, affirmations, and positive self-talk, special forces operatives are trained to build a strong, resilient mindset. These methods help them envision successful outcomes and maintain a confident outlook, even in the face of daunting challenges.

During intense training exercises, special forces instructors emphasize the importance of positive reinforcement by celebrating small victories and progress. This approach not only boosts morale but also reinforces the operatives' belief in their ability to overcome obstacles. By focusing on achievements and maintaining an optimistic attitude, soldiers learn to manage stress and maintain focus under pressure. The continual encouragement and constructive feedback create an environment where operatives feel supported and empowered, which enhances their readiness for actual combat operations.

In preparation for battle, special forces units also use simulations and stress inoculation training to reinforce mental fortitude. These exercises are designed to replicate the high-stress conditions of real combat, allowing soldiers to practice staying calm and collected while reinforcing their self-confidence. Positive reinforcement during these simulations helps operatives develop coping strategies and mental toughness, essential for making critical decisions in the heat of battle. By fostering a resilient mindset through positive mental reinforcement, the U.S. military Special Forces ensure that their personnel are not only physically prepared but also mentally equipped to face the complexities of combat with resolve.

In the years that followed, James Donovan's story became a cautionary tale, a symbol of the mind's immense power over the body. Soldiers spoke of him in hushed tones, a reminder of the importance of mental resolve in the face of unimaginable fear.

James's family, devastated by his loss, found solace knowing that he had faced his last moments with courage and clarity. They remembered him not as a victim of the cold, but as a man whose mind, though powerful and brave, had ultimately betrayed him. His story acts as a testament to the strength and fragility of the human spirit, reminding us that the greatest battles are often fought within the confines of our own minds. In the end, it was not the cold that had claimed him, but the icy grip of his own thoughts.

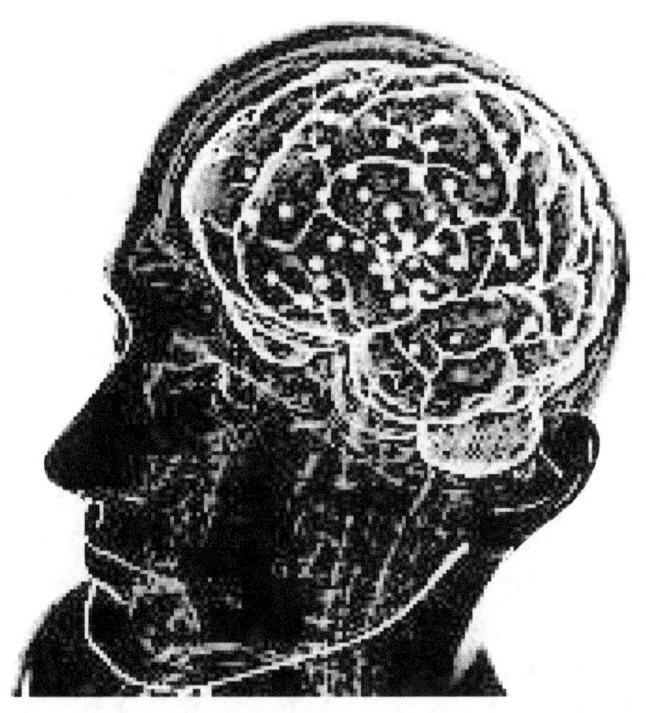

While this is the first time in documented history that a mind caused a death by freezing, Sgt. James Donovan had been killed by his own mind, a prisoner of his deepest fears and darkest imaginings. His death was a testament to the fragile line between reality and perception. The power of the human mind to affect the body and its function is documented. For Sgt. James Donovan of the US Army his delusion became his reality.

# A Rolling Refrigerator... with a Swastika!

Since the early 1900s Refrigerator railroad cars ("Reefers") were used to carry food, that needs to be kept below the outside temperature. Sometimes the insulation allowed the contents to be kept from freezing, such as potatoes. Throughout most of the steam-era, the refrigerant was ice. But melting ice water would spoil foodstuffs, so the ice had to be kept separate. Wood sheathing for reefers was the norm for about two decades after box cars switched to steel because wood was a better insulator than metal. Eventually they realized that steel was better at keeping the insulation in the walls dry because wet insulation stops insulating.

Reefers could carry milk, produce, or meat. Milk and produce had to be kept COOL, meat had to be kept COLD. In order to lower the melting point of ice below 32 degrees, salt was mixed in (just as it is used to melt ice on sidewalks). But the resulting brine was extremely corrosive to steel, including steel rails like railroad tracks. This was a challenge because ordinary reefers allowed the corrosive meltwater to drain out of the bottom of the car.

These new 'Kulwagens' boxcars were mechanical marvels that were truly remarkable. Designed to maintain a steady temperature, they transported

priceless cargo. Both the supply lines and the front lines were getting longer and more dangerous with each passing day. The front lines were located a great distance from the fertile fields of Germany. The refrigerated vehicles were an essential component of the war effort of the Reich, serving as a vital artery of the Nazi war effort.

The German Wehrmacht faced a number of formidable logistical issues, and they built these train cars to overcome those obstacles. It's a combination of technological skill and practical need. The engineering that went into their creation was complicated, although their design was minimalistic it was fully functional. The exterior of a Kühlwagen was strong, made from reinforced steel and wood to endure the rigors of wartime travel. The construction of these train cars aimed to withstand the worst conditions, from the frigid expanses of the Eastern Front to the bomb-blasted rails of Western Europe. With steel walls several inches thick, they were meant to offer both structural stability and insulation. This insulation was essential in preventing external temperatures from affecting the perishables.

At the core of the Kühlwagen was the cooling system. Powered by a small diesel engine, these systems included compressors, evaporators, and condensers, working in concert to circulate refrigerant and remove heat from the interior. The temperature inside the boxcars was carefully controlled, and it was typically kept at about 2-3 degrees Celsius (36-38 degrees Fahrenheit). A temperature chilly enough to preserve food, but also above freezing, so as not to damage the precious produce, poultry and meat. Each Kühlwagen was also equipped with a sophisticated temperature monitoring system. Thermometers were strategically placed throughout the car to ensure a consistent climate. Crew members can view these measurements at a glance from outside, and modifications can be made to the cooling system to maintaining the required temperature.

Operating one of these boxcars needed a team of committed staff. Engineers and mechanics were responsible for maintaining the cooling systems, ensuring that the diesel engines were functioning smoothly and that the refrigerant levels were appropriate. Regular inspections and maintenance procedures were necessary to prevent spoilage.

Introducing the Kühlwagen had a profound impact on the German army's logistical capabilities. Before their deployment, supplying fresh food to the front lines was a near-impossible task. Perishable goods would spoil long before reaching their destination, leading to food shortages and malnutrition among the troops. The ability of the German army to transport fresh provisions over vast distances and the delivery of high-quality food to its fighting forces even in the most remote and hostile environments was instrumental in increasing moral and fighting effectiveness..

Engineers made consistent improvements to the design of the Kühlwagen in order to make it more resistant to these dangers. As the war progressed, engineers made improvements to the protective measures, as well as developed more effective cooling systems and insulation materials. These innovations not only enhanced the performance of the Kühlwagen but extended its lifespan.

As the war drew to a close, the Kühlwagen remained a symbol of the German army's logistical ingenuity. Though many of these refrigerator cars were repurposed or scrapped in the post-war years, their legacy endured. The principles of mobile refrigeration and efficient supply chain management developed during the war continued to influence civilian logistics for decades to come.

The Kühlwagen were more than just vehicles; they were a testament to the power of innovation in the face of adversity. They showed that even in the darkest times, human ingenuity could create solutions that not only met immediate needs but also laid the groundwork for future advancements. In this way, the Kühlwagen transcended their role as wartime tools, becoming enduring symbols of resilience and progress. These cars were more than just a logistical innovation; they were a lifeline, a symbol of ingenuity in the face of adversity.

The Kühlwagen came to be seen as a symbol of German technological advancement and inventiveness over even the most difficult war obstacles. The success of the Kühlwagen was not without challenges. The Allies, recognizing their importance, targeted the refrigeration trains in bombing raids and sabotage missions. Partisan fighters ambushed supply convoys, destroying tracks and derailing trains. The German High Command responded by increasing security with armed guards reinforcing the rail lines.

# WWII FACTS & FIGURES

The second world war happened between 1939 and 1945. It's believed that between 70 and 85 million people died, which is roughly 3 percent of the approximately 2.3 billion people who were living on Earth at the time.

Numbers show that between 50 and 56 million people lost their lives as a direct result of the conflict, including both military and civilian casualties. It's also estimated that between 19 and 28 million people lost their lives as a direct result of the war-related diseases and disasters.

Despite the fact that only 2 million of the more than 16 million Americans who served in the war did so in Europe, the conflict against the Nazi's occupies a very disproportionate amount of space in the American psyche. But it's incredible how many people from the USA had enlisted, since there were around 140 million people living in America in 1945, this means that an amazing 11.3% of all Americans served.

Those who served are an aging population. It's estimated that overall today's veterans are 65 years old on average. Veterans who served after September 11, 2001 have a median age of around 37 years old, soldiers who served during Vietnam have a median age of approximately 71 years old... in WWII its approximately 93 years old.

It's believed that nearly one million Allied forces participated in the Battle of the Bulge, including 500,000 soldiers from the United States.

On the battlefield, around 19,000 American soldiers were killed, while another 47,500 were injured and 23,000 were reported missing in action.

• Over 1,000,000 miles were marched during the Battles in Italy and Sicily.

• Next to Normandy. France, Bastogne, Belgium is the most visited World War II battle site.

• There were only 20 major battles in Europe

• Soldiers had toilet paper ration of 22 sheets a day

• The December 1944 re-supply was one of the largest air drops of the war with a record 240 planes dropping more than 1400 bundles of supplies into a one square mile area.

• During the some parts of the war America soldiers were down to a few bullets each.

- It's estimated that had the German Tanks had another 100,000 liters of fuel they may have achieved their goal and won the war.

• During the some parts of the war America soldiers were down to only a few bullets each.

Here are some other fascinating WWII figures:
Total Deaths = Approximately 22-25 million
Wounded = 25,000,000
Civilian deaths = 45,000,000
Refugees = 16,000,000
US troops dead in World War II= 405,399
German Military Deaths = Approx. 5.5 million
Russian Deaths = Estimated at 20 million
Japan Deaths= Estimated at 2.6 million
Aircraft Produced = 916k
Tanks = 280k
Artillery = 257,400
Warships = 1410
194 countries participated
Total deaths: Approx. 60 to 70,000,000
Total Cost of the War: $125-150 trillion
Marshall Plan to rebuild Europe = $12 billion

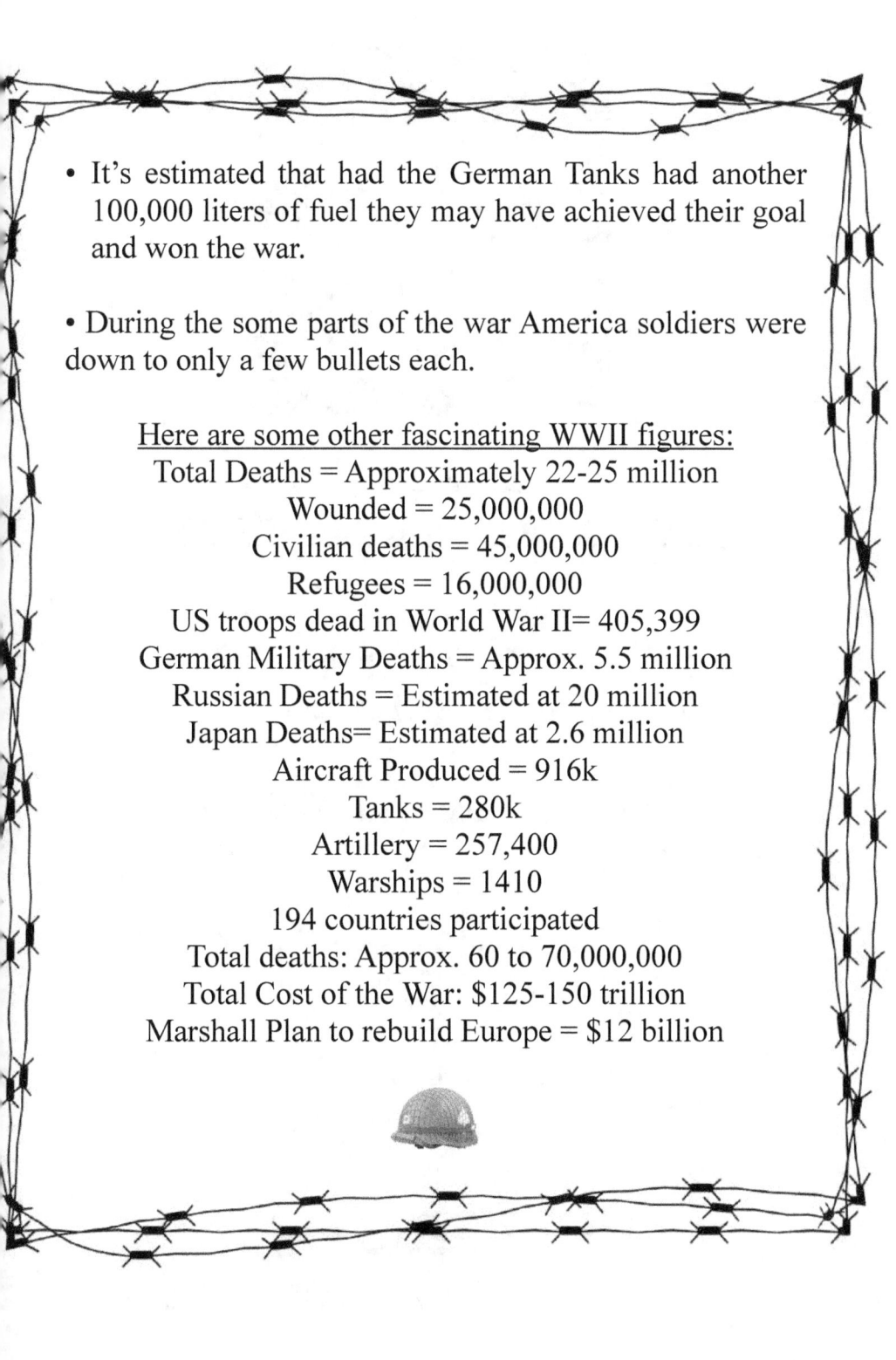

## Please Visit:
## www.authortommcauliffe.com

Please send questions to:

*Bookinfo@nextstopparadise.com*

## *Please Leave a Review!*

*Member:*
Alliance of Independent Authors
Florida Writers Association
Emerald Coast Writers
Military Photojournalist Association
Michigan Writers

# INFO SOURCES

https://www.nationalww2museum.org

https://www.bandofbrotherstour.com

https://www.asomf.org

https://armyhistory.org

https://americanveteranscenter.org

https://navalaviationmuseum.org

www.archives.gov/research/military/ww2

http://ww2.vet.org

https://www.worldwar2salute.org/

Top 100 WWII Movies
https://www.imdb.com/list/ls059324807/

https://www.uap.org/post/top-military-museums-to-visit-in-the-us

https://www.loc.gov/collections/world-war-ii-maps-military-situation-maps-from-1944-to-1945/about-this-collection/

# <u>Acknowledgments</u>

*Veterans from all wars who have stepped forward to defend our nation!*

National World War Two Museum

The Estate of Tommy McAuliffe

US Army Public Affairs, Washington DC

WWII Historical Society

National Holocaust Museum

DepositO Photos

101st Airborne PAO, Ft. Campbell, KY

University of Michigan, Neurosciences Dept.

Izzy Grace Editorial Services

Mr. John Yost

# Books by Author Tom McAuliffe

- **Mr. Mulligan** - *The Life of Champion Armless Golfer Tommy McAuliffe*

- **Nuts!** - *The Life & Times of Gen. Tony McAuliffe*

- **Throttle Up** - *Astronaut Teacher Christa McAuliffe*

- **Mad Dog!** - *Detroit Tiger Dick McAuliffe*

- **Charmed** - *From Motown to Combat & Back*

- **Almost** - *The Road to the Grande*

- **Thunder Road** - *Goodyear, God & Gatorade*

- **Buddy, Brian and Me** - *A Spooky RnR Story*

- **Frozen** - A *WWII and Mind over Matter Tale*

- **Soft Shell** - *Teddy the Talking Turtle*

- **Max and Me** - *Paws Across the Water*

- **Off the Rock** - *Escaping Alcatraz*

## Books - eBooks - Audiobooks

*On sale at Amazon, Kindle, Apple iBooks, Barnes & Noble and your local independent book store.*

## Also Available at:
### WWW.AUTHORTOMMCAULIFFE.COM

MAX
AND
ME
*A Story of Hope*

YA

**Tom McAuliffe**

From the Award Winning Author of Mr. Mulligan

OFF
THE ROCK
Escaping Alcatraz

**Tom McAuliffe**

From the Award Winning Author of Mr. Mulligan
Volume 1: The McAuliffe Series

Detroit Tiger
Dick McAuliffe

MAD
DOG

**TOM MCAULIFFE**

Buddy
Brian and Me

Star Bar

Tom McAuliffe

SOFT SHELL
TEDDY THE TALKING TURTLE

YA

**Tom McAuliffe**

ALMOST
*The Road to the Grande*

Detroit Bands of the
mid-to-Late 60's
You Almost Remember!

TOM MCAULIFFE

THUNDER
ROAD

GOODYEAR, GOD
& GATORADE!

TOM
McAULIFFE

FROM THE AWARD WINNING AUTHOR OF "MR. MULLIGAN"...
NUMBER 3 IN "THE MCAULIFFE SERIES"

TEACHER ASTRONAUT
CHRISTA MCAULIFFE

THROTTLE
UP!

TOM MCAULIFFE

MR. MULLIGAN
*The Life of Champion Armless
Golfer Tommy McAuliffe*

FROZEN
*A WWII Mind Over Matter Tale*

**Tom McAuliffe**
From the Award Winning Author of Mr. Mulligan

FROM THE AWARD WINNING AUTHOR OF "MR. MULLIGAN"

CHARMED
FROM MOTOWN TO COMBAT AND BACK!

TOM MCAULIFFE

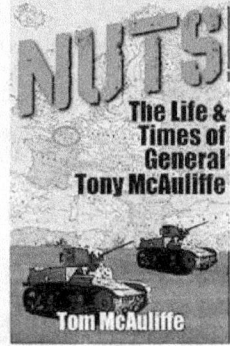

NUTS!
The Life &
Times of
General
Tony McAuliffe

**Tom McAuliffe**